THE
TENNIS
MACHINE

THE TENNIS MACHINE

by Helen Hull Jacobs

Charles Scribner's Sons
New York

To my sister, Jean, with love

1 "I'm scared." Little Tony Mercati looked down across the roofs that fell like steps from the apartment house on Jones Street to the bottom of the hill at Taylor Street. Far beyond the roofs, the Ferry Building stood like a peaked sentinel over the placid waters of San Francisco Bay. He felt as if he were being asked to fly from here to there. His voice was reedy with fear. On the street corner below, Vicky Clifton had gathered her team. They always challenged Dave Thomas's team to a game of "heats" on Saturday afternoon, and Tony had felt very courageous and eager for the test Vicky had decided to impose upon them. As a rule, she chose lower ground for this glorified game of hide and seek, called "heats." But today she had looked up at the tallest apartment building and had said, "We'll start there—on the roof—and we'll jump across all the way down the hill, and then we'll hide in the basement of the last apartment."

It had sounded very daring. Dave's team, on the corner a block west, giving Vicky's team a ten-minute head start before beginning the pursuit, would never expect them to jump the roofs.

It was only when Tony looked down and saw the outline of the first light well that his heart began a strange pounding.

"Don't be a creep!" Vicky told him, and her green eyes flashed with disgust as they did at any sign of weakness or fear in others. "We told you if we let you play you couldn't back out and give us away." She turned on the others, grouped behind her wiry, imperious, twelve-year-old figure. "You're not afraid, are you?"

They shook their heads. Eddie Marsh, 14, looked worried, with a serious frown on his flushed face. Jeanette McGraw, 11, nodded hesitantly, for her gangling body was as filled with fear as Tony's ten-year-old heart. Kathryn Gates, 12, shook her head in rapid, emphatic jerks, lest any of them doubt her courage because she was slender and soft-skinned and had an angelic face that all boys seemed to fall in love with on sight. Roger Halloran, 14, responded with a casual, self-confident shrug, as if this were no different than sauntering home from school.

Vicky looked at them with a slow smile of approval, as if their negation of fear vindicated her choice of them as a team and of herself as their leader. "See!" She threw the word at Tony, who wasn't looking at her. His large, dark eyes, usually soft as pansies and shining with some inner delight, were searching the faces of the others like a terrified small animal's. He found no comfort in them. The faces seemed to blend and blur, and the bodies beneath them to grow taller and menacing. Under Tony's crisply curled black hair his scalp prickled.

"All right," he said in a low, defeated voice.

"Come on, then. I'll lead." Vicky wheeled to face the first jump, the sharp planes of her cheeks and chin bold in the early autumn sunlight. A breeze stirred a few bronze strands of her hair and swept them back from her face. Poised to run, she started from the back edge of the roof and raced across the sanded tarpaper. At the far edge she leaped, arms spread wide. Easily negotiating the seven-foot breadth of light well, her body propelled forward in its descent to the next roof. Barely hesitating, she ran on, hearing behind her the pounding of feet and thump of landings. When she was airborn, she felt a wonderful exhilaration, as if she had sprouted wings and could fly, if she chose, straight across the city, and the bay, and land gently on the brown Berkeley Hills beyond.

Three roofs down, the light well looked wider, and she gave an extra hard thrust as she leaped. Beneath her, she sensed the dark chasm and saw the unexpected roof ledge with a quick, strange fear—not for herself, but for Tony, with his short, pudgy legs and fear already in his heart. When she landed, she turned, breathing hard, to yell a warning and wave the others back. But they were half a roof's length behind her, and in their excited shouting to one another, they paid no attention. She watched, still now. A cold inner trembling shot up her legs to the pit of her stomach. Suddenly it seemed as if the sky were cut by legs, flying in scissor motion, spanning the abyss, straining to a landing. First Roger's, then Eddie's, followed by Kathryn's, then Jeanette's, and finally the tense, spread-eagled legs of Tony, terror in his eyes and tight little mouth. The final, frantic thrust of his legs was not enough to propel him over the edge of the roof. In a moment of silent horror, they heard his scream and saw him hit the ledge, bounce from it, and crumple on the roof.

Vicky was the first to run to his side. Tony's whole body was distorted, his left arm and hand bent grotesquely beneath him, and a bone protruded from his bleeding wrist. Vicky choked back a surge of nausea.

"You did it! You made him jump!" Jeanette's voice

3

was the first that came through to her, shrieking. "You bullied him into it."

Vicky looked up at her. She saw her drawn, thin face and bloodless lips. "You killed him!" Jeanette condemned her again, and in a moment she was fleeing to a doorway and the stairs leading down to the street.

"We didn't do it. Jeanette's right . . ." Kathryn cried.

"Is he dead?" Eddie asked in a whisper.

"I don't know." Vicky's voice trembled.

"Look at his arm. It's all broken."

"I know."

Two spots of color burned in Eddie's cheeks. Trickles of perspiration slid from his temples. He brushed at them roughly and stared at Vicky. His eyes had gone a slate gray, without a trace of their usual bright blue. "We can't just let him lie here!" His voice rose, breaking.

"We're not going to," Vicky said.

"I don't want to touch him. He's dead," Kathryn wailed suddenly. "I can't."

She's weak and ugly now, Vicky thought, in a flashing impression of tears and soft flesh melting together.

"You couldn't help, anyway," she said to the hysterical girl.

"Take me home, Roger, please!" Kathryn tugged at Roger's arm. He shook her off.

"Go home by yourself."

"I'm afraid to. My mother'll kill me. You can tell her what happened. She'll believe you. Please!"

"Shut up!" He whirled on her. "You think I'm going to leave Vicky and Eddie to do it alone?"

"Do what?" she screamed.

"Get him out of here—take him home!"

Kathryn's voice dropped to a whisper. "I can't help, I

can't touch him," she repeated. Her hands trembled against her face, muffling the sobs that came in wracking gasps.

"Take her home, Roger," Vicky said. She didn't think that Roger would be of any help, either. She could see that for all his being so sure of himself, his hands were shaking at his sides.

"I won't do it."

"Do what I say!" Vicky cried, but Roger stayed, hovering over her and Eddie. Kathryn hung back behind him, her face still buried in her hands, tears seeping through her fingers.

Vicky turned back to Tony. "Help me turn him over, Eddie." Together, gently, fearfully, they moved the hunched shoulders toward them, turned him slowly onto his back, and heard him groan.

"He's alive, Eddie! He's alive!"

The door to the roof was flung open and through it came a heavyset man in soiled overalls. "What're you doing up here?" He moved with a menacing scowl toward the group and then his eyes fell on Tony, and he froze in his steps. Kathryn dropped her hands from her face and moved to the door.

Vicky stood up, looked at the beard-stubbled face, the black, fixed eyes. "He's hurt bad. Will you help us?"

"What happened? What were you doing up here?"

"Just help us, will you?" Vicky begged. "We were jumping across the roofs and he hit the edge and fell."

"I get the police!" The man started for the door.

"No!" Vicky cried, her heart thudding wildly.

"Don't do that, mister. Please!" Roger pleaded.

"Maybe he'd better," Eddie said, and his friends looked at him as if he had betrayed them. "They'll take him to the hospital. He has to go there."

"Maybe he doesn't!" Vicky cried. "We've got to get him home. Mrs. Mercati'll get a doctor. We haven't any right—"

"I get the police," the man repeated harshly. "It hurt him more if we move him. There might be something else wrong with him. He doesn't look good—not just a broken arm." He looked at all of them again, in turn. "You stay here—you got plenty to explain to the cops."

Vicky faced the hostile glare. "We weren't going to run away."

"You bet you don't." He narrowed his eyes and added warningly, "I watch the stairs."

When he turned to go, they realized that Kathryn was no longer with them. As the heavy footsteps faded, Vicky said scornfully, "I'm glad she went. She's a coward. Standing there bawling. She didn't care at all about Tony."

"We're sure in trouble." Roger's ashen face looked stricken.

Vicky wheeled on Eddie. "Why did you agree with that man?"

"I had to. He's right," Eddie answered in quick self-defense. "We learned that in first aid. You're not supposed to try to move them when they're hurt bad. You're just thinking of yourselves," he added.

"I'm not," Vicky cried, and sat down beside Tony, brushing a few matted curls off his damp forehead. She tried not to look at his arm. The little boy's soft cries were like accusing fingers, jabbing at her. She bit her lip and wondered if God would punish her for this.

The three fell silent, waiting for the sound of footsteps on the stairs. Roger, sitting down at Tony's feet, kept his eyes on the open doorway.

The sound of a siren, whining in the distance, then growing closer, brought them to their feet. They looked at each other, nervous, frightened, unprepared for what happened when the police took over. Stiffly, they faced the door and heard the clattering on the stairs. Two ambulance attendants in white came through the door with a stretcher, followed by a policeman and a man carrying a doctor's black bag. Finally, lumbering after them, came the man who had called them.

The policeman and the doctor knelt over Tony as the attendants unrolled the stretcher and placed it beside him. Deftly and gently, the doctor injected Tony with morphine, put a splint on his arm, and nodded to the attendants. They started to lift the boy onto the stretcher. His face twisted with pain and he gave an agonized scream. Then he was still.

"He's fainted," the doctor said. "Be careful of that arm."

Vicky was first to find her voice. "Is he hurt anywhere else?"

The doctor gave her a baleful look. Evidently the man in overalls had told him what had happened. "I won't know till I examine him." He followed after the stretcher.

"Where are you taking him?" she called to the retreating back.

"Children's Hospital," the policeman told her in a quiet voice, and when they looked at each other she could see that he knew they were frightened and wanted to be as nice to them as he could.

"What's the boy's name?" he asked, taking a small, black notebook from his pocket.

"Tony Mercati," Vicky answered.

"Where does he live?"

"Over the grocery store at Taylor and Pacific."

"His father's name?"

"He hasn't got one. He's dead."

7

"His mother?"

"She runs the store. It's hers."

The policeman scribbled rapidly. "Suppose you tell me what happened," he said.

The softness of his tone was reassuring. Vicky looked at the others and at the sullen face of the man who had found them and who stood now at the policeman's side. She saw a little muscle twitch in Eddie's cheek and wondered if he was remembering how she had goaded Tony and if he would tell on her.

"We were playing 'heats'," she began, and paused. The policeman seemed to know what that was. There was no question in his eyes. "Tony begged us to let him play with us—" Her glance slid to Eddie, who nodded and backed her up.

"That's right. He really begged us."

Vicky hurried on. "When I saw how wide the light well was, I tried to stop them all from jumping, especially Tony. But I couldn't. They didn't see me until it was too late. I couldn't help it!" The words seemed to choke her. She swallowed a lump in her throat.

"I'm sure you couldn't," the policeman said.

"They had no business up here, playing that crazy game—tenants downstairs thought their ceiling was coming down—" the man in overalls broke in.

"Never mind, Mr. Peters. I'm handling this." The policeman looked sharply at the stormy face.

"I'm in charge of this building. I got a right to complain. The tenants—"

"I said never mind. You can make your complaint later, if you want to."

The policeman turned back to Vicky. "Go on," he said kindly.

"He landed on that roof ledge and fell." She stopped.

The policeman nodded and pursed his lips. "What's your name and address?"

"Vicky Clifton. 1110 Jackson Street."

"Your father's name?"

"Frank Clifton."

The policeman's brows arched. "Frank Clifton—say, is that 'Bearcat' Clifton?"

She nodded.

"What do you know? Best tackle Cal ever had."

"Do you have to tell him?"

"Not if the boy's going to be all right. But you're going to tell him, aren't you?"

"Yes," she said.

He took the same kind of information from Eddie and Roger, snapped the book shut, and returned it to his pocket. "You'd better get on home, all of you."

"I've got to tell Mrs. Mercati—I live on the same street—" Vicky's voice trailed off. Having said what she must do, the thought terrified her.

"I'm going with her," Eddie announced.

"Guess I should, too," Roger said weakly.

"I don't want you to. I don't want anyone to go with me."

"You do that—it's the decent thing to do," the policeman said. "But I'm going down there right away. Routine. If you want to wait till later, maybe your father would go with you—"

Vicky shook her head.

"There was another girl here," Peters spoke up. "She must have run away."

"Oh?" The policeman's glance questioned Vicky.

"She was scared, that's all," Vicky said.

"What's her name?"

"Kathryn Gates. She lives on Gough Street. I don't know what her father's first name is." She wouldn't mention Jeanette. Mr. Peters hadn't even seen her.

"Well, go along, now." The policeman herded them in front of him. Peters followed. On the first floor he left them, silently, and went to the basement. Down on the street, the policeman got into his car and drove off.

There was no sign of Dave Thomas's team. They must have run all the way down to Powell Street looking for them, by now.

2 "Guess I'll go home if you don't want me," Roger said. Vicky's look was a dismissal, and he ran up the hill.

"What are you going to tell your father and your aunt?" Eddie asked.

Vicky was thoughtful for a while. "Just what happened."

"Everything?" Eddie pressed.

"You mean that I made him jump? That's what you're thinking, isn't it?"

Eddie's face reddened. His blue eyes turned from her direct gaze. He looked down at his feet.

"Well, I won't tell them *that*," she said. "He didn't *have* to play with us," she added.

"What'll they do to you?" He looked at her again.

"I don't know."

"Won't you let me go with you to Mrs. Mercati's?"
She shook her head.

"Then I'll just walk to the corner with you. I wish I could help you—I mean, help you tell Mrs. Mercati—or something—" There had never before been a time when Eddie had a chance to help Vicky. She had never seemed to need anyone to help her in anything. He was always a little in awe of her because she could do most things better than he could. She could beat him at tennis and outskate him. About the only thing he could do better was swim.

She shook her head again. "Thanks, though, Eddie."

She started to walk on, and he fell in step beside her. She didn't speak until they had reached the bottom of the hill. "Do you think I ought to tell Mrs. Mercati it was my fault?" she asked.

"No!" he cried. "It wasn't really. Like you said, he didn't *have* to play with us. He didn't *have* to jump, either. He didn't want to be left behind."

She thought about it. "Maybe not," she conceded.

They came to the corner. "Are you going home now?" she asked.

"If you're sure you don't want me to go with you."

"Are you going to tell your parents?"

"I'll tell my father—"

Eddie was lucky. His father never got mad at anything. If Eddie did something wrong, he gave him a talking to, but he did it quietly. Vicky had met Mr. Marsh at Eddie's tenth birthday party in the big house on Pacific Street. He had come into the glass-enclosed room where they were playing games to say hello to Eddie's friends and to bring each of them little models of one of his ships, the *Santa Clara*, with davits and screws and rudders that worked. He had red hair and blue eyes just like Eddie, but he was as skinny as a stick and he spoke so soft it was hard to hear him. Eddie said he'd been on every ocean in the world.

Vicky's father was quick-tempered, slow to forgive. She loved him, but she stood in awe of him, of his strength, and his rugged face and dark eyes that could burn right through her.

Vicky and Eddie said goodbye, and she walked slowly

around the corner, past her apartment and down Taylor Street. She looked up at the third-floor bay windows protruding like frogs' eyes from the white frame facade. It was an ugly building. She wished she lived anywhere but there. She had hated the apartment ever since her mother had died in it, five years ago. Aunt Nan had tried to make it pleasant for them, but she had a quick temper, too, and she was strict. She was prissy like an old maid, always fussing about how Vicky dressed, complaining if she wore jeans like the other girls.

Ahead of her was the faded brown awning with "Mercati's Grocery" on the side. A long slit in the canvas cut through "Store." Strands of torn canvas hung down from it. Vicky stood on tiptoe, trying to see through the display of cans and bottles in the window to the counter where fat, friendly Mrs. Mercati usually stood. But today, instead of Mrs. Mercati, she saw a stranger in animated conversation with a woman customer. Vicky took a deep breath and walked into the store, waited for the flood of conversation to run out. "Pity, pity." The customer wagged her head. "If I can do anything to help, Mrs. Stefani—"

"Thank you. There's nothing—"

"I'll come by tomorrow."

The customer was gone, and Mrs. Stefani turned sad, black eyes to Vicky. "Yes?"

"Is Mrs. Mercati here?"

"She's at the hospital."

"Oh—"

"Her boy had an accident. My husband took her in his car. I'm her sister."

Vicky debated whether to say to this stranger what she had come to say to Mrs. Mercati. Not all of it, she decided, and said, "I know—I mean I know he was hurt."

"You were there?" Mrs. Stefani came around the end of the counter and stood before Vicky, her thin, hawk-nosed face outthrust.

"Yes," Vicky answered, drawing back.

"He was hurt bad? The policeman who came didn't say—just he had a broken arm. I think it was worse. He wouldn't tell her to get to hospital so quick just for a broken arm."

"That's all I know—his arm," Vicky said. "I'll come back when Mrs. Mercati's here." She ran out of the store, followed by "Wait, wait!" and the hurrying footsteps of Mrs. Stefani. She didn't look back. She ran all the way up the hill, flew across the corner and into the entrance of her apartment building on Jackson Street.

Inside the hall, she stopped to catch her breath. She was lucky that Mrs. Mercati hadn't been there, even if it only put off for a while the time when she must see her and find out how Tony was. She wished she knew, now, that Tony was all right. She'd seen a broken arm once before, but it didn't look like his, bent the way it was and with the bone sticking out at the wrist. And Tony looked so funny—just like Mr. Peters said—at first as if he were dead, and then when he opened his eyes, staring as if he didn't see anything he was looking at, with his face as gray as cement.

She dragged her feet up the two flights of stairs to her apartment. There was no chance her father and Aunt Nan wouldn't be home. On Saturday he always came home from his lumber company in time to watch the football game on TV. And you could set a clock by Aunt Nan. At five, unless they were going out to dinner, which they didn't do often, she would be preparing vegetables, putting them in pots of cold water until time to cook them for six-thirty dinner. Aunt Nan didn't approve of frozen vegetables. She never did anything the easy way.

When Vicky opened the door, she could hear football fans shouting and screaming, and through it she heard the wildly excited voice of the commentator on the TV. Her father was hunched over in his chair in front of the set like a myopic bear. She crept by him, not daring to interrupt him now, and went to the kitchen.

"Aunt Nan," she said at the doorway, in a voice just loud enough to be heard above the din of the television. Her aunt didn't like her coming in without calling. The first time she had come up behind her in the kitchen, Aunt Nan had jumped a mile, then turned on her and shaken her in a fit of nerves. "Don't ever do that again!" she had cried, wild-eyed, and it was some time before she had calmed down. She said she was sorry to have shaken Vicky and yelled at her, but she didn't like to be startled. Vicky had smiled at her, easily forgiving. Aunt Nan was a bag of nerves, she guessed.

Her aunt turned her head from the sink, paring knife poised above a string bean. "Oh, you're home. It's after five. You get cleaned up and—" She stopped in mid-sentence, turned around, and put down the knife. "What's the matter with you? You're pale as a sheet."

"Nothing's the matter with me." Vicky put her hand to her cheek as if she could feel the paleness. "Something happened, though."

"Come sit down." Aunt Nan went to the breakfast table at the window. Vicky sat down opposite her. There was one thing about Aunt Nan. She was strict, but she was kind, and now she looked at Vicky gently, concerned, and urged, "Tell me."

Vicky started at the beginning, emphasizing that Tony had pestered them to allow him to play. When she got to the part where he had said he was scared, she hesitated. Then, "I guess I talked him into jumping," she said, for when Tony was conscious and remembered, that's what he'd say, and it's what the others would say, too. Except Eddie. It was the truth. She didn't have to say she yelled at him, though—told him not to be a creep. She didn't have to make it as bad as it was.

All the time she talked, Aunt Nan's eyes never left her face. Her hands, folded tightly on the table, were still, the knuckles white. When she had finished, Aunt Nan lowered her eyes, her thin brows drew close together, the creases between them deepened. The noise from the television rose, filling the room. She heard her father let out a whoop.

Aunt Nan looked at her. "We'll go to see Mrs. Mercati after dinner—you and I." She nodded toward the living room. "You must tell your father—as soon as the game's over. Don't disturb him now." She got up. "We'll have dinner early. Why don't you freshen up now? The game should be over by then." She put her arm around Vicky's shoulder, gave it a gentle squeeze. "Don't worry." Aunt Nan knew Vicky's father wouldn't take it calmly. Not with his temper, and not when he disapproved of Vicky's tomboy ways. But when he simmered down, she'd have a talk with him. Seven years older than her brother, she'd always had some influence on him.

"That's it. That's the end. I don't ever want to hear of your playing that game again, or nipping cable cars on your skates, or any other damn fool thing you do." Frank Clifton was sitting on the window seat. Vicky, standing stiffly in front of him, stared out at the bay.

"Lower your voice, Frank. Do you want all the neighbors to hear you?" Aunt Nan shifted uneasily in her chair.

He lowered it to a growl. "You're going to act like a young lady from now on. Do you understand? And you'll play ladylike games—not go jumping over roofs like some kind of a tomboy nut!"

"What games?" Vicky asked.

"What's wrong with jumping rope, or even tennis? I bought you a good racket and you've hardly used it."

"Jumping rope's for babies," Vicky muttered, "and there's no one to play tennis with except Eddie. None of the kids—"

"Then play with Eddie." He got to his feet, strode the length of the room, then whirled around. "You and I are going to see Mrs. Mercati—"

"I'm sure she won't be home yet," Aunt Nan broke in. "Anyway, I'm going with Vicky, after dinner."

"You stay out of this, Nan."

"I'll do nothing of the kind. Listen to me, Frank. If there's any comfort to be given Mrs. Mercati, you're in no humor to do it. And you hardly know her."

His smoldering eyes cooled. His face, with its heavy brows, wide, thin mouth and jutting chin, sagged. "Maybe you're right." He sat down, and ran his fingers through his thick hair. "If Vicky's responsible for this, you tell Mrs. Mercati I'd like to take care of the boy's hospital bill. It's the least I can do."

Aunt Nan pulled herself up, bridling. "Do you want it to look as if Vicky forced that boy to jump?"

"She did, didn't she?"

"No, I didn't!" Vicky yelled.

"*You* lower *your* voice," her father ordered.

"I'll find out if there's anything we can do," Aunt Nan said, "but I'll do it my way."

He waved his arms as if to shove away the whole dreadful matter. "Do it any way you like," he said. Then he added, scowling at Vicky, "I meant what I said to you."

Vicky started to speak, saw the warning light in his eyes, and ran to her room.

Aunt Nan sighed and nervously fingered a wisp of blond hair. "You can be grateful she doesn't run around with a pot-smoking bunch—or worse—and that she's honest."

"Vicky and her friends get their kicks trying to break their necks."

Aunt Nan pursued her subject. "You read about that nine-year-old boy who died from an overdose of heroin. At least—"

"All right, Nan. I *am* grateful for that. I don't suppose it ever occurred to me it was possible—not Vicky."

"Don't you imagine that's what all parents think?"

"I get the point." He jammed his hands into his trouser pockets. "But my point is that I don't want her to be a roughneck. I'd like to think that she might grow up to be like her mother."

Aunt Nan shook her head. "She isn't like Eleanor. She's like you—strong, willful, and high-strung."

"What do you mean willful?"

Aunt Nan didn't expand. "Guide her, Frank. But don't try to make her over."

A sudden look of sadness came into Clifton's eyes. No one could be made in the image of Eleanor. If he could have given her some of his strength—she was scarcely larger than a child, her fair, fragile beauty so vulnerable to the illness that took her.

Aunt Nan put her hand on his arm, gave it an affectionate squeeze. "She's a fine girl. Don't worry about her." She went to the kitchen. "Dinner will be ready in five minutes," she called. "Tell Vicky—and *don't* say anything else."

After dinner, Vicky and Aunt Nan walked down to the grocery store. Mrs. Mercati was spending the night at the hospital, but Mr. Stefani told them about Tony. He towered over them, his frowning, troubled face as dark as his unruly hair. "His arm's broke in three places, and he broke his heel. They had to operate on him."

"Oh, Lord," Aunt Nan breathed.

"That's awful," Vicky said, feeling a cold lump in the pit of her stomach. She was waiting for him or Mrs. Stefani to say it was her fault.

"He can't play the violin anymore," Mrs. Stefani added, mournfully. "The doctor said his wrist will be too stiff. It's a shame. His teacher said he would be a very good player."

"I didn't know he played the violin," Vicky said in a scarcely audible voice.

"It's all he likes." Mrs. Stefani spoke as if Tony's life were over, and Aunt Nan said quickly, "My brother— Mr. Clifton wanted me to tell you that if there's anything we can do—we all feel so dreadfully about this—"

"No. There's nothing," Mrs. Stefani said emphatically.

"Tony will be in the hospital some time?"

Mr. Stefani nodded. "Three weeks."

Aunt Nan pursed her lips. "My brother would like to help with the hospital bill—"

Mr. Stefani shook his head. "Thank you—we don't need money—"

"Well, if you find you do—hospitals are so expensive—please don't forget."

"We won't," Mrs. Stefani said, seeming less reluctant than her husband to consider the offer.

"Did Tony tell you what happened?" Vicky asked Mr. Stefani.

"He didn't say anything. He didn't talk at all. But we know."

"I think it was my fault." Vicky blurted it out.

"Don't say that!" Aunt Nan cried. "It wasn't any more your fault than the others. That Halloran boy could have stopped him. He's older than you are and he should have had better sense than—"

Mr. Stefani interrupted. "We don't blame anyone," he said. "None of them had any sense to play that game. Maybe they won't anymore."

"This one won't." Aunt Nan took Vicky's arm in a firm grip. "We'll keep in touch with you to see how Tony gets on." She propelled Vicky toward the door. "When he's well enough, Vicky would like to go to the hospital to see him."

"Yes, I would," Vicky said.

Mr. Stefani nodded.

"And please don't forget—we'd feel better if we could help," Aunt Nan said as they left.

"I didn't know he played the violin," Vicky said again as they went up the hill.

"Would it have made any difference to you, if you had?" Aunt Nan asked tartly.

Vicky knew it wouldn't have. She was leader of the team. All she had thought about was having them do as she said.

3 As he always did on a school day, Eddie was waiting for Vicky at the corner of Larkin and Jackson streets. "I'm glad you came," he said.

"Why wouldn't I come?" She gave him a sharp, challenging glance and quickened her pace.

Reluctant to put thoughts into her head that he was happy to believe, now, were not there, he answered, "I don't know—there's no reason."

She knew what he meant, but she wasn't going to admit to anyone how much she had wished she didn't have to come back to school. Today would be the worst day of all. Tony would be missing at recess, and there would be no tugging at her arm, and the pleading, "Can I play, too, Vicky?" over and over. Tony had never seemed to want to play with children his own age. Once one of the girls had laughed and said Tony had a crush on her. Vicky had looked at her scornfully. For there was quite a difference to her between a silly crush and the admiration she felt Tony had for her.

As they approached the schoolyard, most of the class-bound pupils paid little attention to Vicky. A few cast quick, unfriendly glances at her, then averted their eyes; some scowled at her and whispered among themselves. Vicky figured she could thank Jeanette and Kathryn for the hostility. They'd probably been busy on the telephone over the weekend, and had made it sound even worse than it was.

"Vicky!"

She and Eddie turned at Roger Halloran's call.

"Wait a minute." He trotted up to them. "Did you hear anything about Tony—how he is?" he asked.

Vicky looked at him steadily, suspiciously for a moment. He was Kathryn's friend—hardly her friend at all. Briefly, she answered, "He broke his heel."

Roger's mouth fell open. "Jeez—his heel too."

"What's with everybody?" Eddie blurted. "They're acting like Vicky had leprosy or something."

Roger shrugged. "Word gets around, I guess—"

"What word?" Eddie's face got red, his eyes blazed and he took a step toward Roger.

"You know—" Roger said, and kept an eye on Eddie's tightening fists.

"Like I made him jump," Vicky snapped at Roger.

"I didn't say that," Roger protested.

Vicky thrust out her jaw and leveled her green eyes at him. "No. But you think it and that fink Kathryn probably told everyone." She paused, narrowing her eyes. "Did you tell your parents?"

"No." He bit off the word.

"You were afraid to?" She began to frown.

"I guess so."

"Come on, Eddie," she said, and left Roger standing there as she went into the building.

"Do you want to play tennis this afternoon?" Eddie asked.

"Maybe," she answered. He was really nice to her, she thought. He knew there would be no more games with the others for a while.

"You can tell me after school, Vicky."

"I'll have to go home and get my racket."

"No, you won't. I'll use my father's and you can use mine. We can get them on the way to the court."

"All right."

Outside her seventh-grade classroom, they parted and he went on to his eighth-grade room.

The tennis courts at Lafayette Square were deserted when they arrived after school, and they were able to play for an hour and a half without having to give up the court to waiting players. To Eddie's surprise, he beat Vicky easily, although she seemed to be trying. As a rule, he was lucky to win a set.

"You weren't very good today," he told her when they had finished.

"I know," she admitted. She had tried, for she didn't like being beaten, but she couldn't keep her mind on the game. In the middle of a rally, when she should have been figuring how to outmaneuver Eddie, she had been thinking about how strange school had seemed today and how alone she was now, except for Eddie, of course. In class when she had recited, the pupils around her had kept their eyes on their books, or stared at the blackboard behind the teacher's desk. "I'll be better next time, if you want to play again," she said.

"Sure I do. Let's play every day. It's really more fun than anything else." Eddie stuffed the two tennis balls into his pockets and took the racket from her.

"I'll bring my racket to school tomorrow," she said, and he noticed that her face brightened a little. "I think yours is too heavy for me."

Eddie didn't know whether or not her racket had anything to do with it, but when they played the next afternoon Vicky won as easily as she usually did. They had had to wait for two men to finish playing. While they were warming up, the men put on their sweaters and watched them. Then, instead of leaving, they sat down and continued watching until Vicky had won the first three games. Occasionally the elder-looking of the two said something to the other, who nodded.

"She plays like a boy," the tall, gray-haired man said. "And she's sure giving that young fellow a trouncing."

"I wonder if she plays here often," the other said. "Have you ever seen her before?"

"No, but I'd like to keep an eye on her." He rose from the bench. "I've got to go now, Sam, or I'll miss my train."

"How long will you be gone?"

They left the court together.

"Two weeks."

Eddie was glum as they strolled through the park to the street. "I guess you'll want to find someone else to play with you," he said. "I'm not good enough."

"Don't be a nut," she answered. "I don't always play that well." Then, as an afterthought, she added, "You don't mind being beaten, do you?"

"Of course not!" He stopped swinging his racket and looked at her with offended eyes that had gone very pale blue in his flushed face.

"That's good, because I want to get much better."

"If you do, you'll have to get a pro to give you a game."

"Oh, I won't get that good for a long time," she said. "Anyway, you'll get better. You'll see."

Vicky was right. Pride, and his desire to be an adequate opponent, spurred him to Herculean efforts at steadiness and accuracy for as long as the autumn evening light lasted. After they had played, he went home and hit balls against the garage door. He didn't tell Vicky of his slavish devotion to improvement. He wanted to surprise her and, he hoped, please her with a game worthy of her time. He stole precious moments from his homework to read books he found in the library on tennis by famous players.

While she seemed to know instinctively how to make the strokes so that they were effortlessly produced and apparently correct from his study of slow-motion action photographs, he had to work not to be thrown into contortions, trying to reach some of her shots, particularly those to his backhand. He tried to reproduce the perfect strokes before the long mirror on his bedroom door, book in one hand, racket in the other.

By the time autumn had ended, Eddie was making Vicky work for her victories. But she was still the natural-born player, he the plodder. He could see that.

It was soon apparent to Vicky and Eddie, even on weekends when there were many waiting to play at Lafayette Square, that the tall, gray-haired man was often there and that he watched her with more than casual interest. On a Saturday, when she and Eddie had finished a set and were waiting for their turn to play again, the stranger approached them and said to her, "You play a very good game. Have you been playing long?"

Vicky thought for a minute. "Two years—about." She was trying to remember when she and Eddie had first come to Lafayette Square.

"Do you have a coach?" he asked.

She shook her head. "I just watch the good players and try to copy them."

"You've done well," he said approvingly. "My name's John Bartlett. I'm secretary of the Northern California Tennis Association. You might say we run tennis in this part of the state. That is, we organize the tournaments and make the rankings, among other things," he explained.

"I've never seen a tournament," she said. "Have you, Eddie?"

"No," he replied, "but I'd like to."

"What are your names?" John Bartlett asked.

They told him, and he promised to see that they got tickets to the next big tournament in the spring. Then he asked Vicky, "Do you mind if I make a suggestion?"

"No. I want to learn everything I can."

"You must practice on placements. Put a piece of cardboard or a handkerchief in, say, the backhand corner of the court and practice until you can hit it every time. Then put it in a corner of the service court, the forehand corner, and so on—"

"But Eddie and I like to play sets—"

"You can still do that, but spend half of your time on placement practice. You can both do it—make a game of who can hit the mark most often."

"The other people who are waiting to play might not like it," Vicky suggested.

"You have a right to use your playing time any way you want," he said. "Would you like to be a champion?"

"I guess I would," she said. "I never thought about it."

"I think you can be. But it's hard work, you know. There's more to it than the strokes."

"What?" Vicky asked.

"I'll send you a book that will answer that question, and it'll help you if you'll study it carefully."

The court he was waiting for was free. "Don't pattern

your game after mine," he laughed, and joined three players for doubles.

It amused Vicky that Mr. Bartlett, who had advised her about her game, was himself such a poor player. He hit the ball like an old woman, and when he ran, he looked as if he might fall on his face. But what he had told her made sense.

Two days later, when she came home from the courts, the book was waiting for her. It was heavily wrapped and Aunt Nan hadn't opened it, but she was curious about it and about the sender, whose name and address were on a corner of the wrapping.

"Who is this Mr. Bartlett?" she asked, as she handed the package to Vicky.

"A man Eddie and I met at the tennis court," Vicky told her while she tore eagerly at the wrapping.

Aunt Nan was almost as impatient as Vicky to see what the book was. She couldn't imagine what sort of book a stranger would send to a young girl, or why he would send one at all. She was relieved when Vicky exposed the title: *Match Play and the Spin of the Ball* by William T. Tilden, 2nd, and she looked over Vicky's shoulder as she turned the pages. There were diagrams of a tennis court, dissected by straight and broken lines and curves; there were action photographs of players making shots from various positions on the court, and pages and pages of text. Vicky's head spun. Was there this much to know about the game?

"This is terrific!" She clutched the heavy book close to her. "Mr. Bartlett said I could be a champion if I'd learn to hit the handkerchief every time."

"What *are* you talking about, Vicky?" Aunt Nan asked, totally confused. She knew nothing about tennis and, in any case, didn't see what a handkerchief could possibly have to do with the game.

Vicky explained and added, as if she were quite familiar with the organization, "He's secretary of the Northern California Tennis Association."

"Oh, I see." Aunt Nan began to understand. "He watched you play and thinks you play well—and wants to help you. How nice of him."

Vicky thought her aunt underestimated his opinion of her. "He said I could be a champion," she repeated.

"Wouldn't that be nice," Aunt Nan said, almost indifferently. It disturbed her that tennis seemed to have put Tony out of Vicky's mind. She certainly didn't want her to brood over the boy's accident, but when she herself had called and reported to Frank and Vicky that Tony was in pain but was doing satisfactorily, Vicky had seemed to take the news as a release from responsibility.

"Before you start your homework—and I don't mean reading that tennis book," Aunt Nan said firmly, "I want you to call Mrs. Mercati."

Vicky looked cornered. "What'll I say?"

"Ask how Tony is, of course. And ask when you can go to see him in the hospital."

"Aunt Nan, I don't think I want to go to the hospital," she said, and at the expression of rising displeasure on her aunt's face, she hurried on. "I know I said I wanted to go, but I've been thinking."

"What?" Aunt Nan snapped.

"I don't think Tony would want to see me."

"That's for Mrs. Mercati to say. I'm sure if Tony doesn't want to see you, he'd tell her. Now, you phone her."

Vicky dropped her head and stood, for a moment, staring at her toes. Then, slowly, she moved to the phone, looked up the number, and dialed.

"Mrs. Mercati this is Vicky Clifton and I want to know how Tony is," she said in one breath.

"Oh. He's doing all right. Not quite so much pain now." Mrs. Mercati spoke tonelessly.

Vicky was conscious of Aunt Nan's attentive ear. "Would he like me to go to the hospital to see him?" she asked. There was a long pause. "Mrs. Mercati, are you there?"

"Yes. I told him you wanted to come see him. I'm sorry. He doesn't want you to."

"He doesn't?" Rejected, Vicky felt guilt stirring again. "Please tell him I'm glad he's getting better," she said weakly, and hung up.

"He doesn't want to see me," she said to Aunt Nan, and went to her room. Forgotten was the tennis book. She tried to do her homework, but couldn't keep her mind on it. She was staring out the window when her father came into her room.

"Aunt Nan told me about your talk with Mrs. Mercati," he said. "You did what you should—to ask when you could see Tony. Now I want you to remember that he's still a sick boy, Vicky. When he's well, I'm sure he won't feel this way."

"He always will," she answered.

Her father put his arm across her shoulder and kissed the top of her head. "Don't think about it. Promise me." He couldn't press his point for he wasn't really sure that she was wrong. "Promise?"

She nodded.

"Worrying won't do Tony a bit of good," he added, and then said, to change the subject, "Aunt Nan tells me you've had a compliment about your tennis. That's fine."

"Uh-huh," she answered. It didn't seem very important now.

4 As the weeks went by and Vicky's game improved, so did Eddie's. But he was still unable to beat her, or even to press her very hard. She had read and digested Tilden's book, and concentrated so much on every point she played that she rarely spoke to him during the set. He began to feel as if he were playing a robot.

One Saturday, toward the end of the year, Mr. Bartlett brought a serious-looking young man with him to the courts. He introduced him to Vicky and Eddie. "This is Bob Carter. He's a member of the San Francisco Tennis Club. Would you mind playing a few games with him, Vicky?" To Eddie, he said, apologetically, "I don't mean to be unkind, but you really aren't good enough to push her."

"I know that," Eddie said, and frowned dejectedly at the blunt appraisal of his game.

"But I like to play with Eddie," Vicky said.

"Of course you do," Mr. Bartlett hastily agreed. "But I want to see how you play against someone who's better than you are."

"I'd like it very much," Bob Carter said. "Mr. Bartlett says you have the makings of a champion."

"Go on, Vicky," Eddie urged.

"I don't think I'll be very good against you," Vicky warned.

She wasn't, at first. The ball came from Bob's racket with more speed than she had ever seen, and its pace off the court was so swift that she had hardly begun her forward swing when it was past her. Once Bob stopped play to explain to her that she must start her backswing as soon as the ball reached the net. "Then you must hit it as it comes up off the court," he went on. "That's called hitting the ball on the rise. You borrow speed from your opponent's shot, hurry him, and often catch him off balance. And it's your best chance to pass him at the net before he can get to the ball. If you wait for it to start dropping, you'll lose a lot of power and give your opponent a chance to get into position."

He slackened the pace of his shots a little while she tried to adjust her timing, and it pleased him to see how quickly she learned.

As she raced from side to side, her white pleated shorts flying, and the bouncing locks of her hair shining like burnished copper in the warm sunlight, she realized what Mr. Bartlett meant when he said that Eddie wasn't good enough for her. She had never before had her strength and endurance tested like this. When she came to a standstill at the end of the rally, she was breathing in quick, shallow gasps.

"Want to stop for a minute?" Bob asked.

She shook her head. As soon as she got her second wind, she'd be all right, she thought, but she was still gasping when they finished the set. "You've had enough for today," Bob insisted. "You ought to do a lot of deep-breathing exercises."

They walked to the bench where Mr. Bartlett sat with Eddie. "That's a great improvement," he said, getting to his feet. "Taking the ball on the rise—you must practice that all week. We'll be back next Saturday. All right with you, Bob?"

"Sure is," the young man agreed, and he gave Vicky an admiring smile.

"We'll have to sharpen up your net game and that second serve of yours. Do you walk to school?" Bartlett asked.

"Yes—why?"

"Try jogging for a block or two, breathing deeply. You've got to build up your stamina along with your game."

Eddie, who stood listening, broke in with an embarrassed smile, "I can't hit anywhere near as hard as Bob. Don't you think Vicky ought to get someone else to practice with her during the week?"

Bartlett shook his head. "You're steady now. That's important. And don't forget—Vicky's going to be playing against girls in tournaments. I don't mean to offend you—" He gave a little laugh and put his hand on Eddie's shoulder. "I'm speaking of very good girl players. But they don't have Bob's speed, either. They don't have Vicky's speed, for that matter, so she's got to learn how to hit the slower ball on the rise, too. It's harder to hit a slow ball on the rise than a fast one."

"You get that down pat and increase your accuracy on the short crosscourt shots and you'll have the girls in the grinder," Bob promised her.

5 One evening in early May, John Bartlett called on Frank Clifton. Vicky, studying in her bedroom with the door closed, was unaware of his visit. When Aunt Nan suggested getting her to join them, Bartlett replied that he would rather talk to Frank alone first. Aunt Nan tactfully withdrew to the kitchen, and Frank made a drink for Bartlett and himself.

"I'll come straight to the point, Mr. Clifton. I think your daughter's going to be a great tennis player. She needs competition, and I'd like to enter her in the Pacific Coast Juniors in June."

Frank gave a low whistle. "Hold on there, Mr. Bartlett. You're going too fast for me. I haven't seen her play, but she can't be that good."

"She is," Bartlett said. "I think she can win it."

Frank leaned back in his chair, twisted his glass in his hand. "This is quite a surprise. I knew she liked the game. She plays every day it doesn't rain. But that's always been rather like Vicky. She sets her mind on something and hangs onto it like a steel trap. But then she loses interest, and that's the end of it."

Bartlett was not to be discouraged. "I don't think she'll lose interest in this. She has an extraordinary talent. Her strokes are flawless as far as I can see. I've had one of our best players from the San Francisco Tennis Club playing with her, and he agrees. She's ready."

Frank looked at him seriously. "I've been an athlete myself—football was . . ."

"Well, I'll be damned. You're *that* Frank Clifton—the Bearcat—" Bartlett grinned. "That makes things a lot easier. We can talk the same language—competition, that is. I was never much of an athlete myself, but I've had a lot to do with tennis champions."

"I don't know a thing about tennis, but I guess I know what it takes to win in any sport."

"Of course you do. Then you agree?"

"I think we ought to ask Vicky."

"You won't find any opposition there, I'm sure," Bartlett said confidently.

"I'll get her, and my sister would like to hear about this, too." He opened the kitchen door. "Come on out, Nan. We have something to tell you. I'm going to get Vicky."

Aunt Nan turned the burners low under the vegetable pots and joined Bartlett. He rose. "I didn't mean to exclude you, Miss Clifton. It was Vicky—" he started to explain, apologetically.

Aunt Nan waved it aside. "I had to start dinner, anyway. Won't you stay and have it with us?" She sat down at the end of the sofa.

"Thank you. I'm afraid I can't. I shouldn't have stopped by at this hour, but I was passing the apartment on my way home and I thought I'd catch Mr. Clifton."

"You live nearby?"

"No. I live just a block from Lafayette Square. That's how I happened to meet Vicky. I usually play tennis at the club, but occasionally I use the courts there."

"You've been very kind to Vicky—helping her with her

game and giving her that book. I can assure you she appreciates it. I don't know a thing about tennis. I don't think Frank does, either. It's nice that someone who does takes an interest in her."

"She's a very promising player. Very," he told her emphatically. "Your brother has agreed to let me enter her in the Pacific Coast championships."

If he had said Frank had agreed to let her sing at the San Francisco Opera House, Aunt Nan would have been no less startled. She sat upright. "Why, she can't do that!" she exclaimed. "She was just thirteen in November!"

Bartlett laughed. "The juniors, Miss Clifton—not the women's." To his relief, Frank came back to the room with Vicky. Her eyes danced with excitement. Bartlett stood up and smiled at her. "You know why I'm here?"

"Oh, yes! I think it's wonderful." She looked at Aunt Nan's solemn face. "Isn't it, Aunt Nan? Isn't it great!"

Aunt Nan managed a smile. "I guess it is, Vicky, if your father and Mr. Bartlett think you should."

"Of course I do," Frank answered. "But she's got to promise not to be too disappointed if she doesn't do well. She's got to be a good loser. After all, her first tournament—"

"It's just as important for her to be a good winner," Bartlett said, and looked at Vicky. "You can't tell how you'll react to winning *or* losing until you've had the experience." He looked back at Frank and then at Aunt Nan. "As a matter of fact, if she had any experience at all, I wouldn't hesitate asking you to let me enter her in the women's singles, as well. I'll go so far as to say that if she proves to have a good match-play temperament she can win the women's nationals in three of four years. Maureen Connolly did it at sixteen."

Frank gave him a steady, sharp glance. "If she's that good, I'll make a champion of her in two years. I know something about psychology in sports, Mr. Bartlett."

"That's pushing her a bit," Bartlett said uneasily. This might not be good, he thought. Tennis wasn't football. You didn't play eyeball to eyeball, threaten your opponent with extermination, batter him with brute force. Psychological strength in tennis wasn't the same thing that it was in body-contact sports. He might have trouble with Frank Clifton. Vicky would have to learn for herself a stern kind of self-discipline and self-control. Her father couldn't do that for her. But he could make her too tense, and too anxious.

Aunt Nan frowned. They were both pushing Vicky. She was so young. She could be easily discouraged if they expected more of her than she could do. If she could just have played in some minor tournament first—

"We've got a lot to do before June," Frank Clifton said, rubbing his hands together.

The faintest frown crossed Bartlett's face. Aunt Nan saw it. Frank didn't.

Vicky looked at her father, puzzled. She didn't see how he fitted into the picture. He didn't know anything about tennis.

"Where is the tournament?" Frank asked.

"The Berkeley Tennis Club. It starts the fourteenth and runs through the twentieth."

Frank took a small engagement book from an inner pocket of his coat and noted the dates. "I'll plan to be free then," he said.

"I have one more thing to discuss with you." Bartlett leaned forward in his chair. "It's not absolutely necessary, but I would like to see Vicky join the San Francisco Tennis

Club. We have an excellent pro there—Jerry Potter. There would be the expense of becoming a member, but I've talked to Jerry and he would like to coach Vicky free of charge. She needs a good coach now. Someone who can refine her game, teach her strategy and tactics. That young friend of Vicky's—Eddie Marsh—just isn't good enough any longer. Bob Carter can give her stiff practice on weekends. He works during the week. It would be an ideal setup for her."

Vicky's face clouded over. She would like to belong to the club. She wouldn't have to change her clothes in the school gym any longer, and she probably wouldn't ever have to wait for a court. And she was sure a pro could teach her a lot. But what about Eddie, who had worked so hard to help her with her game? They were pushing him aside as if he didn't matter.

Her father noticed her frown, her lack of enthusiasm. "What's the matter with you, Vicky? Don't you want to join the club?" He barked the questions impatiently at her.

"Sure I do," she answered. "I was thinking about Eddie—"

"Don't think about anybody else—but we'll talk about that later." To Bartlett, he said, "I'll be glad to have her join. It makes sense to me. But it isn't necessary for the pro to coach her for nothing."

"He wants to. It's not unusual, Mr. Clifton. It means a great deal to a pro to help develop a champion. You can understand that."

"I suppose so," Frank conceded, but it went against the grain for him to be beholden to anyone.

"How far away is the club?" Aunt Nan asked.

"Not far from Vicky's school—California and Larkin," Bartlett told her.

"That's nothing, Aunt Nan." Vicky wondered if her aunt was going to object to everything. "I can take the cable car to Larkin and it's only four blocks to California." She paused. "And after school's out, I can play earlier and I won't be so late getting home," she added, suspecting that this was what bothered Aunt Nan.

Aunt Nan nodded but said nothing, and Bartlett hurriedly asked, "Then it's settled?"

"Yes, it's settled," Frank agreed.

"I'll make the arrangements." Bartlett rose. "Vicky, you can plan to start playing there the first of the week. Come straight to the club after school. Jerry will be waiting for you." He looked at his watch. "My Lord, it's seven o'clock. I must apologize for keeping you good people from your dinner so long." He stood up, and the others rose with him, Aunt Nan a little too quickly.

"Doesn't matter a bit," Aunt Nan said politely. "I'm sorry you can't stay."

When Bartlett had left and Aunt Nan had scurried to the kitchen to prepare the lamb chops, Frank looked solemnly at his daughter. "Sit down. I want to talk to you while Aunt Nan's getting dinner."

"Maybe I can help her." Vicky didn't like the look in her father's eye. It was only there when she had done something to displease him.

"She can manage alone." He sat down opposite her in the bay of the window, his large hands folded between spread knees. The final, pale light of evening played across his rugged face, lit his eyes. "I know how you feel about Eddie, but I want you to understand that if you're going to take tennis seriously—and I presume you are or you wouldn't be joining the club—you're not to think of anyone but yourself and your game. There's no room for sentiment, or concern about how Eddie's going to feel. He isn't good enough practice for you, so that's that. You go on to someone who can help you."

"But he's my friend," she protested.

His dark gaze flickered impatiently. "Of course he's your friend, but he has no place in your game."

She shifted uneasily in her chair. She couldn't toss Eddie aside like that.

"Tell me," he said. His tone dropped, pinioning her attention. "Do you want to be a tennis champion? I don't mean just a junior champion. I mean the national champion."

"I guess so."

"You guess so!" He shot to his feet, jammed his hands in his trouser pockets, stared down at her.

"Yes, of course I do," she said quickly.

"Then remember you've got to eat, sleep, and think tennis." He jabbed the air with his forefinger. "I know what I'm talking about—"

"What about school?" she threw at him.

"That's what I was going to ask you," Aunt Nan said from the kitchen doorway. "Come on. Dinner's ready."

They went to the dining room. "That's a stupid question," Frank grumbled.

"I hope so," Aunt Nan replied, "because nothing is going to interfere with her schoolwork."

"I didn't expect it to. She'll go to the club, play, come home and study." Frank kept his eyes on his plate.

"And never see her friends?" Aunt Nan asked.

"I don't have any—except Eddie," Vicky blurted, "and now I won't have him, if I can't—"

Frank interrupted her with an impatient wave of his

hand. "Don't be silly, Vicky," he said shortly, "you'll see him at school." He cleared his throat, changed the subject. "I'd like to borrow your tennis book."

"Sure, Dad. But why?"

"I want to read it," he said.

"A little knowledge is a dangerous thing, Frank," Aunt Nan reminded him in a chiding tone.

He ignored her remark. "I know teaching you the mechanics of tennis is up to the pro, but I want to learn as much about them as I can, Vicky, so I can speak your language and understand your game. I'm going to drill you in what I think is eighty percent of winning—the three C's: confidence, concentration, and consistency. That's my field, Vicky. It made me an All-American. When you've got the equipment you need in the way of strokes and shot-making, that's when I step in."

"But you can't make me have those things," Vicky reasoned.

"I can."

The explanation she waited for, eyes fixed on her father's face, was not forthcoming. Instead he said, "After you've had a few lessons with the pro, I want to watch you play. I want to see what kind of a game you have. The mental approach you need depends on that—as it does in any sport."

"Don't you think you'd better leave that up to the pro, Frank?" Aunt Nan asked.

Clifton silenced his sister with a glance. ". . . Like the tackle versus the quarterback." He picked up the thread of his thought and was off on the love of his athletic life. Vicky listened with half an ear. Power against speed and finesse, defense against offense. She listened without hearing now. She was thinking about Mr. Bartlett, who played like an old woman but had helped her game. At least, he played tennis. Her father didn't know a forehand from a backhand. Silently, she finished her dinner as Clifton droned on.

"It's eight o'clock." Aunt Nan interrupted her brother's monologue. "Vicky has got to do her homework."

"Okay, okay." He pushed back his chair. "Bring me that book before you start, will you, Vicky?"

Later, when Vicky came to say good-night to Aunt Nan and her father, he was sitting in his chair by the window reading Tilden. Aunt Nan smiled at her and gave her a surreptitious wink before Clifton looked up from the words of tennis wisdom.

For the first time since she'd known him, Vicky felt embarrassed with Eddie. It was Friday, their last day of tennis together, and she didn't know how to tell him without hurting his feelings. Saturday and Sunday she was playing with Bob, and then Monday she was going to the club to begin working with the pro.

She played poorly, let Eddie run her around aimlessly, and made errors in judgment and timing. Suddenly he caught the ball and went to the net. "What's the matter? Don't you feel like playing?"

She walked slowly up to join him and he saw in her flushed face and unhappy eyes that something was wrong. "Are you sick?" he asked, worried.

She shook her head, and then the truth poured out. He stood there, motionless, a frown around his eyes. When she had finished speaking, waiting for him to say she didn't know what, he said simply, "I guess they're right."

"But I don't want to stop playing with you, Eddie."

"I wish I were better," he said. Then knowing that he

shouldn't let her see how disappointed he was that all his hard work on his own game had been for nothing, he tried to whip up enthusiasm. "Even if I were, I don't know enough about tennis to do you any good." A smile crept over his face. "It's great, joining the club and having a pro to teach you. I can see why they want you to have one if you're going to be a champion."

"Maybe I won't. Maybe they're all crazy. How do they know I'll be a champion? I have *fun* playing with you."

"I think you'll be a champion, too," he told her matter-of-factly. "You don't play like most girls—that's why. But I guess it's hard work, and not much fun until you're on top." Her green eyes looked misty. He'd never seen her cry. He hoped she wasn't going to now. He wouldn't know what to do. Quickly he suggested, "Why don't we finish the set?"

She walked back to the baseline. Her eyes began to clear. She'd gotten over the painful hurdle. Eddie wasn't as upset as she'd thought he would be.

6 Vicky was unfamiliar with the tournament players, and didn't recognize the slender, blond-haired girl, six years older than she and several inches taller, who was coming off the court with Jerry Potter. They stood talking at the courtside bench and she stopped a little distance away from them until Potter saw her and beckoned to her.

"You must be Vicky Clifton." He smiled and sized her up in a quick glance from sturdy legs to bronze head.

"Yes, I am." She was surprised to find him short and tending to a paunch. Thin, sun-bleached hair plastered to his head was partially covered by an eyeshade, and plump cheeks drooped into the beginning of jowls. He was not what she imagined a tennis pro should look like.

"We're glad to have you here," he said, and turned to the girl beside him. "I want you to meet Chris Stafford." He expected the name to mean something to Vicky, but realizing that it didn't, he added, "Chris is the California State women's champion."

"Hello, Vicky." Chris put out her hand to Vicky, who was observing that the champion didn't look strong enough to be the best player in California.

Vicky found her voice. "Hello," she said, took the surprisingly large hand, and felt its firm grip.

"I hear you're a very good little player." Chris's deep violet eyes were friendly and, Vicky thought, the most beautiful she'd ever seen.

"I've asked Chris to play a few games with you, Vicky," Potter said. "I'd like to see how you handle yourself against her."

"I'm not good enough, yet," Vicky demurred nervously.

"That doesn't matter. This is only for fun. Maybe I can give you a few pointers." Chris took her arm and drew her toward the court. Potter took up a position at the net post.

As they began to play, Vicky's nervousness wore off, and she felt that she was hitting the ball well in corner to corner exchanges. But something was happening when she tried to go to the net. Chris was hitting the ball in a way that made it drop sharply crosscourt at Vicky's feet. She managed to scoop up forehand volleys of these shots, then saw Chris, at the net, slam the high returns past her into the open court. At least, she thought, she had volleyed the ball, but on the backhand, its impact turned the racket in her hand and the attempted volleys were flubbed into the net. Potter shook his head.

"Stay back for a while," Chris called to her, and Vicky felt a flush of mortification. The champion didn't think she could play net. But she could if Chris would hit the ball straight instead of playing those shots that dropped heavy as baked apples almost onto her shoe strings.

Vicky went obediently to the backcourt. Again, the exchanges from corner to corner, and she felt that she could hold her own until, suddenly, Chris hit a short crosscourt drive that flew off Vicky's left service court corner. Wildly she lunged for the ball, stabbed at it, and her return floated over the net. Chris let the ball go and spoke to Potter. "Do you mind if I show her the grip?"

"Go ahead. You've got one of the best backhands in the game."

"What's the matter with my grip?" Vicky asked, holding it out for inspection, fingers and thumb wrapped around the handle.

As Potter watched, Chris took the head of the racket and moved it until it was perpendicular to the ground. "Keep your grip," she said, as Vicky withdrew her hand. Chris put her palm against the strings. "Now, see if you can keep me from pushing the head back."

Vicky stiffened her wrist, exerted all the pressure she could, but Chris pushed the racket head back with ease. "You see you have no support with that grip. Now put your thumb diagonally across the back of the handle and push against my hand again." The racket head went back, but slowly this time, and Vicky could feel her thumb resist the pressure. "See? Your thumb not only supports the racket against the pressure of the ball, but it helps direct it. Let me show you how the stroke ought to be made." She demonstrated—elbow leading until the forearm moved forward to the hitting position, shoulders pivoting with the stroke, body weight moving from left to right foot. "You do it, now."

Vicky emulated Chris as closely as she could, but the stroke felt awkward.

"You're pretending you're hitting a ball at your side," Chris pointed out. "You've got to hit it in front of you— about a foot. And you're bending your wrist forward before your racket reaches the hitting position."

Vicky looked at her bleakly, discouraged.

"Jerry can teach you that in an afternoon. Then all you need is practice on it. Your other strokes are good."

"They are?" Vicky accepted the compliment eagerly.

"Very. All you need to learn is how to use them."

All? Vicky thought. That seemed to grow to mountainous proportions as she recalled how easily Chris had won the four games they had played. She was glad her father hadn't been here—or Eddie—or Bob. She guessed Bob had made her look good on purpose—given her shots she could hit.

"We'll play again, someday," Chris said and left, and Vicky's lesson with Jerry began. The pro wheeled his cart of balls onto the court.

She hit nothing but backhands for an hour, from every position in the court against hard, flat drives and against dropping crosscourt shots like Chris's that Jerry explained were hit with topspin. Before the lesson ended, she felt at home with the stroke.

When they had finished, he told her, "As they say in the theater, you're a quick study. Starting tomorrow, we'll concentrate on placements—every one in the bag—on service and groundstrokes and volley—and we'll get a change of pace in your game. That's important—"

And right out of Tilden's book, she thought.

"You've got to be able to do anything you want to the ball —hit it flat, with overspin, slice—and know when to use each one. And you'll have to learn the lob. That can be an offensive as well as a defensive shot. When you've got all this, you'll be more than ready for the juniors. Think you can learn it all in five weeks?"

She looked bewildered. "I'll try."

"You're a worker, I can see that. And you're strong." They walked back to the squat, white stucco clubhouse together. "You've got a big thing in your favor, Vicky. You know how to take the ball on the rise. Where'd you learn that?"

"Mr. Bartlett told me how, and I practiced it a lot."

"He did!" Potter laughed. "You never know about these old gentlemen. They're smarter than you think, sometimes."

She wondered if that could apply to her father, too.

As soon as Vicky heard her father come into the apartment that night, she left her homework and hurried to the hall to meet him. Aunt Nan had been interested in her meeting the California champion and in her lesson, but Vicky could see that her excited description of the technical things she had learned were over her aunt's head. She thought she could explain to her father, especially if he had read Tilden's book.

"Guess who I played with today!" Bright-faced, she accosted him as he was putting his hat on the rack in the closet.

"The pro, I hope," he answered, and turned to give her a light hug and a kiss on the forehead.

She kissed his cheek in return, then drew back to watch him closely as she told him in a ringing voice, "The woman champion of California. And she said I had a good game. She said my strokes were *very* good."

She waited for him to beam with pleasure, to tell her that was great. But something was wrong. The corners of his mouth tightened. He walked into the living room, carrying the evening paper, Vicky trailing him. "What about the pro?" He swung around.

Vicky regarded her father with a puzzled frown. It was several moments before she answered, "He gave me a lesson afterwards."

"For how long?"

"An hour," she said softly, crushed by his indifference to her exciting news.

"You're sure?"

She nodded.

He went to his chair by the window. The evening light behind his large head threw his face in shadow. "Come here, Vicky, and sit down," he said.

Aunt Nan poked her head around the kitchen door. "Evening, Frank," she said.

"Hi, Nan," he responded shortly and turned his attention to his daughter. Aunt Nan looked from one to the other, took in Frank's scowl and Vicky's frown, and withdrew. Whatever argument they were about to have, she wanted no part of it.

"I don't want you to play with any girls or women in practice," Clifton dictated.

Vicky protested, "She's the best woman player in California, Dad—"

"I don't care if she's the best player in the world. I want you to take your lessons with the pro and play with Bob or any of the other good men players at the club. But no girls—no women. Is that clear?"

"Why?" Vicky wanted to scream the question, but she made an effort to keep her voice down.

Ignoring her question, he went on, "And I don't want you to be buddy-buddy with any of them. You keep your distance and work on your game."

"I don't see why."

"Because if they know you too well, they're not going to be afraid of you. And that's what I want. *I want them to be afraid of you.*" He jabbed his forefinger at her. "Do you understand?"

She bit her lower lip and stared at him.

"All they'll know about your game is what they see when you play with men. They won't know what it's like to come up against you until they do it in a tournament when it counts." He delivered himself of his reason and leaned back in his chair.

"Suppose Chris asks me to play again?"

"Tell her your father wants you to practice with men—lay the blame on me." He flipped open his paper and gave it a cursory glance.

"Dad, I can't. She helped me. She showed me how to hold my backhand."

"What's the matter with the pro?" He looked at her over the top of the paper. "Doesn't he know?"

"Sure, but—"

"No 'buts.' I mean what I say, Vicky." He added, coming suddenly to the decision, "I'll go to the club tomorrow afternoon and watch you have your lesson, and I'll have a word with Potter. That'll make it easier for you."

He was going to spoil everything—absolutely everything. And what would Chris think of her? That she was ungrateful, that she thought she knew it all now, that her father was a kook—

Her father turned back to his paper and she, dismissed, went to Aunt Nan in the kitchen, flopping into the chair by the window. "Dad won't let me play with Chris anymore." Her voice was small and hard as the bitter glare of the overhead light. "She helped me. She probably has a lot of pointers she could give me."

Aunt Nan turned the hamburgers, put a lid on the pan and faced Vicky. "Dear, if you explained to me, I'm afraid I wouldn't understand. Why don't you be patient with him? He might be right."

Vicky stared at her, not rudely, but thoughtfully. Aunt Nan just didn't understand.

Vicky hoped fervently that her father had not come with her to the club to check up on the pro and embarrass her. Since she had lent him Tilden's book, he was always questioning her about the strokes and footwork the pro was teaching her. He seemed to have absorbed Tilden's emphasis on footwork and quoted endlessly from the text. As far as she could tell, everything the pro was teaching her was right there in Tilden's book, but she was nervous, nevertheless, and introduced him to Jerry Potter with misgivings.

"I'm glad you came," Potter said to Clifton. "I hope you'll see improvement in her game."

Clifton gave him a sheepish smile. "I've never seen her play," he confessed.

"You haven't! Well, then, you're in for a pleasant surprise."

"Don't build me up too much," Vicky pleaded, for her father's presence made her feel fidgety and she wasn't sure she'd play her best.

"I won't. We'll show him. Come on."

Clifton took a seat on the bench and Potter dug into the cart for three of the newest balls. "We'll play a set to start with," he said, and gave her a glance that promised he would make her look good.

Afterwards, her father seemed to look at her with new respect, and the only question about her game he asked Potter was, "Do you think she's ready for the tournament?"

"She will be," he replied. "By the way, she ought to have another racket—same kind, same weight, balance, and handle—before then. It's not safe to have just one racket, in case it breaks."

"How about those metal rackets I see advertised?" Clifton asked.

"Too fast for her to change to, now. After the tournament, if you want to get her one—"

"I don't suppose you could pick a racket out for her—"

"Sure. I stock them in my shop."

"Better get it now, then," Clifton said.

Vicky felt that she had taken her first step toward being a champion—two matched rackets.

"I'll have it strung for her by tomorrow."

"Mr. Potter, there's one thing I want to get straightened out about Vicky's practice," Clifton said.

"What's that?" Potter's blond eyebrows rose. He had had prior experience with tennis fathers and mothers, and he was prepared for almost anything—sensible or outrageous.

"I want Vicky to confine it to men opponents, or boys who are better than she is."

Potter sent Vicky a sidelong glance, saw her stiff little figure in its agony of embarrassment. "That's a good idea," he said levelly.

"You'll explain it's *my* wish, if Miss Stafford asks Vicky to play again," Clifton requested.

"I don't think that's likely to come up. I asked her to play with Vicky. You see, Chris has a great backhand—she's a female Don Budge on that stroke. I was hoping she'd see Vicky's weakness and show her how to correct it. Kids are often more impressed when a champion shows them what to do than when the pro does. And that's what Chris did."

Vicky saw that her father was flustered and, in his turn, embarrassed when he interrupted Potter's toneless explanation. "I appreciate it. So does Vicky. She came home all excited about it. It's just that I have a theory, Mr. Potter—"

Potter nodded. "I think I know what it is. It isn't new, Mr. Clifton. Chris would be the first to understand. She doesn't practice with women either. But quite often she helps the young players."

"Well—fine, then—" Clifton fumbled, and quickly changed the subject. "I see you've got Vicky working on the all-court game. I was reading in Tilden's *Match Play*—"

"Dad!" Vicky pleaded, "Mr. Potter knows."

"A great book," Potter said. "Tilden must have been all they say he was—those who know, who saw him at his best—a complete master of the game."

Potter's next pupil, a small boy, came down the walk. "I have another lesson. Will you excuse me?" He seemed to welcome the diversion.

Vicky took her father's coat sleeve. "Come on, Dad. I've got to take a shower. You can wait in the lounge for me."

"See you tomorrow, Vicky." Potter's tone implied, "Alone, I hope."

7   On her way to the club the day school ended for the summer vacation, Vicky felt a stronger sense of freedom than she had at any other term ending. But this had been different from any other term. Except for Eddie, who had continued to meet her at the corner of Jackson and Larkin Streets and carry her tennis bag to school, she had had nothing to do with her former "heats" team and little to do with anyone else. In every eye, even those that would have been friendly, she had seen, or thought she had, the stern sentence of guilt. And so she did the simplest thing: she avoided any intimacy with them.

Little Tony had missed so much school that he didn't come back until the spring term and his class had gone on without him. So there was this to add to Vicky's certainty that no friendly overture, no plea for forgiveness on her part would be welcome. At recess, she kept to herself, doing as much homework as she could to cut down the evening's studying, for she had other tennis books to read. But she had often watched Tony, no longer flitting around the yard like a hummingbird, but trotting clumsily after his friends, his legs no longer sturdy after weeks of inactivity, and his small face much thinner and less childlike. Sometimes, she thought he looked like a little old man. She tried not to let her eyes dwell on his left arm and the disfiguring scar.

Now, it was over, and she wouldn't see any of them. And in just three days the tournament began.

Jerry had lined up a half-dozen young men, in addition to Bob, to play two sets with her every day after her lesson. He would stand at the net post, never moving his eyes from her, observing the slightest flaw in her strokes or tactics as her opponent for that day went all-out against her. The next lesson would be devoted to correcting the flaw: throwing the ball too low on service; forgetting the hop-skip to get into hitting position after running to wide shots; not bending her knees enough on her volleys; trying an impossible line passing shot instead of lobbing. Jerry never seemed to miss anything.

Today, she was playing Mike Wilson, her toughest opponent, and her father was coming to watch. She was used to Clifton's presence now, and so was Potter. If Clifton had any comments to make on her game, he made them at home where he could reinforce them with references from her tennis books, all of which he had read. He didn't seem to want to get into an argument with Potter about anything.

"I want you to serve and go to the net on every service game," Potter told her. "And if you can, Mike, play her crosscourt on every return."

So that was the pattern of the two sets, and Vicky, for the first time, won one of them.

"You're ready, and then some," Potter said afterwards, and Mike added, "She ought to be playing in the women's."

Clifton got up from the bench and sauntered over to the three at the net. The one thing he had looked for today, he had seen. Vicky had stamina. Although she had followed Potter's instructions, her breath came easily. Serving and running to the net, lunging for one sharp crosscourt return after the other hadn't visibly tired her, and she was serving as hard at the end as she had at the beginning. She looked keen and she played that way.

"Well, how did you like that?" Potter asked him.

"Fine. I'd like you to cancel her practice for tomorrow and Sunday."

"Why's that?" Potter questioned. "I was planning a light tune-up for her—"

Clifton shook his head. "I don't want her near the court until her match on Monday. We'll take a drive into the country—have a picnic over in Marin—forget tennis."

"Dad, please. I don't want to do that. I want to practice," Vicky objected.

"You're keen. I want to keep you that way."

She looked to Potter and Mike for support.

"I know you better than they do," her father reminded her, impatiently.

Potter shrugged. "She's your daughter."

Mike said nothing, but he smiled sympathetically at her. Tennis fathers were a breed he had seen in action before.

Vicky cheered up some when Aunt Nan agreed with her father about taking two days away from the court. If her aunt, who didn't seem to think much of tennis, except as a now-and-then pastime, was concerned about her being sharp for the tournament, then her opinion must count for something. "She hasn't done a blessed thing but have tennis drummed into her for nearly eight months. I should think she would be sick of it before the tournament's half over if she doesn't have a break. I'll fix a nice picnic lunch." Aunt Nan gave Vicky an affectionate pat on the shoulders. "I wouldn't even read about tennis if I were you. Just see if the tennis clothes I bought you are all right. They're hanging up in your closet."

Vicky rushed off to look, and behind her the telephone rang. Clifton picked it up. Bartlett's voice boomed over the line. "I expected to watch Vicky play tomorrow, but Jerry tells me she isn't coming to the club."

"No. Nor Sunday," Clifton answered.

There was a pause. Clifton covered the mouthpiece with his hand and said to Aunt Nan in a low voice, "Bartlett."

"Jerry thinks she should, and I want to see how she's doing. I may have one or two things to tell her." Bartlett's voice had lowered, but it was petulant.

"I don't think so. She'll be a lot keener if she has a couple of days off. I thought I made it clear to Jerry that was the way it was going to be—" The firmness of Clifton's tone was not lost on Bartlett.

"I know you did. But I'm asking you to change your mind about tomorrow. She can take Sunday off." Now his voice had the ring of officialdom.

"We're taking her on a picnic. It's settled," Clifton stated.

Bartlett's voice rose again in anger. "Is this part of your psychology?"

"You can call it that," Clifton answered.

"I think I've had more experience in this—" Bartlett began.

"I didn't know you'd played competitive tennis."

"I haven't. But that's beside the point."

"I don't think it is," Clifton contradicted. "I've had plenty of competition, and I know a couple of days change of scene is the best thing for her."

"Football has nothing to do with tennis," Bartlett shouted, and met Clifton's calm reply, "Depends on how you look at it. Anyway, it's settled. So there's nothing to argue about."

Bartlett hung up, and Clifton looked at the phone a moment, shaking his head slowly, pursing his lips before he put it down. "He'd like to run the show," he said, half-aloud.

"He won't have it in for Vicky, will he?" Aunt Nan asked.

Frank looked at her thoughtfully. Only two spots of color in his cheeks betrayed his aggravation. "She's going to be good enough so it won't matter. But no," he added, "I don't think he will. He'll have it in for me. I had a feeling he did after our first talk."

Aunt Nan went back to Vicky's room to see how she liked her new clothes. She wondered what Eleanor would have thought of all this, having been the sort of person who hated any kind of unpleasantness. She didn't think it was a very auspicious beginning for a tennis career, if that was the future Frank had in mind for his daughter.

As if by tacit consent, neither of them mentioned the call to Vicky.

8 Although she was only a junior, Vicky's name dominated the headlines after her first three matches in which she allowed her opponents a total of four games. "Net Prodigy Flashes Across Tennis Horizon," blazoned one, and when Vicky appeared for her fourth match—the round of eight—at eleven o'clock in the morning, she found that it was scheduled for the grandstand court.

Clifton, watching his daughter dispose of her bewildered opponents, realized that she was everything the papers almost rapturously claimed her to be. But what he took most pleasure in was the reporters' astonishment at the unruffled court behavior of the thirteen-year-old. "She seems to be totally unaffected by the gallery," wrote one, "and neither an error—and she made few—nor a bad call made the slightest dent in her composure or her confidence."

Clifton had made a strong last-minute point of his three C's, reiterating them as he had sat opposite Vicky at the living room window, the morning sun streaming across her tense face, while they waited for Aunt Nan to finish dressing. "Concentration: see the gallery as so many heads of cabbage; ignore the personality and behavior of your opponent. I don't care if she stands on her head. Don't let *anything* break your concentration. Pretend you're playing

Bob or Mike, and keep your game to the level you would against them. Consistency: take as much care with the easy shots as the hard ones—never miss a set-up. Confidence: don't let any thought enter your mind except 'I am going to win. I cannot be beaten.' And a forbidden C: no conversation with your opponent—no chit-chat at the net as you change sides."

Then finally, as he had walked to the court with her, "You have the strokes, you know how to use them. Go out there and do it."

He had hoped it had all sunken in and taken hold, but only her opening match, as a newcomer, would tell—and it had. Even Aunt Nan, deposited on the clubhouse porch in a chair in view of the court where Vicky played her first match, had found it hard to believe that the imperturbable, skilled, and merciless girl on the court was the Vicky she lived with. Fearless, yes, and dogged in her determination —she had expected that. But she was unprepared for the game her niece played and the manner in which she played it. Neither a smile nor a word broke the frozen concentration on her face until the match was over, and there was little of either then. Following her father's instructions, she had gone immediately to shower and change, and then, together, they had all watched the other matches for a while and gone home. Frank hadn't even seemed concerned, she thought, about Vicky's next opponent. He maintained that whatever her weaknesses were, Vicky would discover them in the first game. She was trained to ferret out and exploit weakness.

But it disturbed Aunt Nan that in this victory pattern of Frank's, there was no place for friendship. Among all those nice young people, there should be some to replace the friends Vicky had lost at school. Frank's idiotic dictum that she was not to be "buddy-buddy" with any of them prevented this. Surely, with a game as good as hers, she could win without being so cold and aloof. It had been almost embarrassing to watch her silent annihilation of her hapless opponent. The girls on the next court said a word or two to each other when they paused at the net as they changed courts; or mumbled, humanly, to themselves; or let out little shrieks or shook their heads in disgust at poor shots. But not Vicky. She was like a machine, running on ice water. Wouldn't the natural, high-strung temperament inside that wiry, thirteen-year-old body build up pressure and explode before this was all over, shattering the illusion Frank had created and making the bump back to reality tragically hard for Vicky?

Vicky, however, was reveling in the discovery that her father had been right. After the opening set against her first opponent, after the initial nervousness that she couldn't confess, the clammy palms and fluttering stomach had all vanished, her cool had been an easy thing to assume. The routing decisiveness of the 6–1 second set brought a look of helplessness, if not fear, to her opponent's eye. It all worked out as her father had said it would. She hugged the new armor to herself and was content to follow every line of the pattern he had drawn.

Another of Clifton's decisions was that she read nothing of her matches until the tournament was over, and the stack of daily papers that grew during the week was off-limits to her.

When reporters interviewed her after her third match, her father was at her side, and being a famous athlete, he was at ease with them and answered most of their questions for her. They hadn't looked as if this endeared her father to them. Of course, he couldn't say how she *felt*. Did she feel as calm as she looked? Wasn't she nervous at all? And when she answered "no," one had turned to her father and observed that she was pretty young to be so phlegmatic. "As I remember the story," he had added, "you didn't get the nickname 'Bearcat' on account of your cool. Does she take after her mother?"

"No," Clifton had said, truthfully. "I guess she's just herself." Not for anything was he going to crack the illusion, and he had sighed inwardly with relief that Vicky wasn't going to either.

Clifton was waiting for her when Vicky appeared on the porch of the rambling, gray-shingled clubhouse, neat and trim in her white pleated shorts and shirt, her hair secured by a narrow blue ribbon that matched the cuff on her socks. He escorted her to the court enclosure where Bartlett and Bob stood leaning against the box nearest the gate.

Vicky and her father greeted them, Vicky hoping they would tell her they were proud of her progress in the tournament. But if they intended to, her father gave them no chance. Just inside the gate, her stocky, dark-haired opponent, Polly Perkins, waited, eyes wide and curious on Vicky, and Clifton waved his daughter on.

"Good luck," Bob and Bartlett called after her, and drew a muttered protest from Clifton who didn't want Vicky to get it in her head that luck had anything to do with winning. He wondered what Bartlett would have to say now about the match-play psychology he had made light of on the telephone. But all he said was, "She must be playing like a house afire, from all accounts."

Bob beamed his pride in her.

"She owes you both a lot," Clifton acknowledged, and excused himself to find a seat in the stands near Aunt Nan, pleased that he had prevented Bartlett from offering Vicky any advice about playing the girl whose game he probably knew. He wanted Vicky to find out for herself the best way to play her opponents, for unless she could, she'd be at sea against a player who changed her game in mid-match. And that's what a smart opponent would do, if she had been playing a losing game.

Vicky allowed herself a quick glance at the stands and the double tiers of boxes along the clubhouse side of the court. It seemed that there was not an empty seat, and yet it was only midweek. She wondered if all these people had come just to see her play. She wondered if what the papers had said had brought them crowding to her court.

In swift appraisal of her opponent Polly Perkin's figure, she noticed her short, over-muscular legs. She'd never be nimble enough to chase a drop shot really close to the net, then turn and run for a lob to the baseline; nor be fast enough to go for a short angled drive on the right and get back in position to take a deep line drive on the left. During the warm-up, Vicky thought of a half-dozen combinations of plays that could win this match without trouble.

The only thing that puzzled her was that when Polly had won the toss, she chose side instead of serve. But as they neared the end of the warm-up, the reason seemed clear. Polly hoped to break service before Vicky was completely loosened up. There couldn't be any other reason to give up the advantage of the opening serve. She's crazy, Vicky thought, if she thinks that will work with me. And when the umpire called play, she took her place on the baseline and gathered herself confidently to teach her opponent a lesson.

Serving hard and wide to the forehand corner, she went

to the net to volley the return to the backhand baseline corner. But Polly didn't drive her return. Instead, she lobbed high as Vicky rushed in. Caught in mid-stride, Vicky pivoted on one foot, raced back, tried to reach the ball to smash it before it hit the fence. Heavy with overspin, it hopped away from her after the bounce.

Vicky returned to the baseline, leveled a momentary gaze at her opponent and said to herself, "See if she can lob off the backhand." She served wide to that side, going to the net more slowly, anticipating the lob. Polly stooped to the low ball, swung her stocky body into a crosscourt drive and delivered a shot that passed Vicky cleanly. The gallery exploded and Vicky watched the ball roll into the corner.

Love-thirty. Outwardly calm, Vicky felt an unfamiliar flutter in her stomach. This wasn't in her plan for the match at all. She hadn't lost a service game in the tournament, so far. Go for an ace, she ordered herself, and hit the serve flat with all her strength down the center line. Polly lunged for the ball, swept her racket upward and recovered her balance to watch the return sail high. Vicky ran back under it, brought her racket behind her head, waited for the ball to drop to smashing height. But overeager, she hit too soon. The ball flew off the top of the racket frame, over the fence and into the court beyond.

Love-forty.

Watch the ball! her tennis sense screamed at her, and another voice said, Polly's better than you thought, and you're playing her wrong. But she didn't know what the right way was. She'd stay back on the next serve and try to figure it out.

In the driving duel that followed, she had the better of it in length and force, but this wasn't the answer either. In spite of her heavy legs, Polly could run.

Aiming too close to the backhand corner line, Vicky overdrove and the game went to her opponent. She looked straight ahead as they changed courts, her eyes focused on the green backstop. Somewhere in the south stands behind her, her father sat. She wouldn't have looked for him if she knew where to find him, but as she turned toward the sea of faces, she wondered if he was nervous or if he had enough confidence in her to know that one service break wouldn't matter. But didn't it? It would mean the loss of the set if she didn't break back. She drew her handkerchief across her brow and eyes, and took her position on the baseline. Until she knew how Polly served, she wouldn't risk standing in on it, although she knew that moving up to take the ball on the rise was usually unsettling to the server.

Polly's serve was hit more for placement than speed, and the spinning shot to the forehand was not to Vicky's liking. Hitting a short crosscourt return, she was wide of the sideline. She's going to soft-ball me, Vicky thought, knowing she would have to make her own pace instead of borrowing speed from her opponent's shot. This wasn't any fun. There was more chance of making errors, more temptation to take risks without reason.

Impatiently, she returned the next serve to mid-backcourt and went to the net—the "center theory" that prevented a line drive. If Polly didn't lob, she would have to drive crosscourt to right or left. Polly drove low to the backhand, but as Vicky prepared to volley, the ball hit the net cord, hovered there for an instant, then dropped into court, unplayable. Vicky stared at it. If the breaks were going to go against her, too, she was in trouble. She felt the tension of the gallery like a physical force, and sensed an unfamiliar tenseness in herself. Two outright errors on return of service gave Polly the second game.

Vicky's mind whirled in confusion. What am I doing wrong? she cried to herself, and sought the answer in the few seconds she had before serving again. Then, like the sun breaking through a leaden cloud, the answer came: Relax and play as if it were Bob on the other side of the court.

And she did, watching the ball with the kind of concentration that had been missing when she allowed her opponent to intrude in it, when she failed to follow her plan of attack and worried about being soft-balled instead of adjusting her timing to the slow pace. Moving in on the ball, taking it on the rise, Vicky met Polly's threat with an avalanche of flat, speeding drives that raked the court from corner to corner, slid crosscourt, and with volleys that shot through every opening. As Polly's racket faltered, so did her confidence. She was no longer able to force Vicky to play her game. Her lobs, defensive, desperate efforts to keep the ball in play, lost their length and Vicky smashed them mercilessly and unreturnably.

Vicky's utter concentration sharpened her anticipation and it seemed now that she was effortlessly there and waiting for every shot that Polly made. Nothing but the ball and the court—a chessboard—existed for her, and only three errors interrupted the pace of winning placements as she piled up points to take the first and second sets in twelve straight games, twenty-five minutes after she had lost the first two.

As she shook hands at the net with her bewildered and disappointed opponent, a self-admonition came quickly to her mind: "Never, ever be overconfident again."

Polly's white lips seemed to be trembling, and she ran off quickly to the clubhouse.

Vicky was glad the applause that followed her from the court was restrained, in kindness to her opponent. A group of well-wishers moved tentatively toward her. Two or three had autograph books in hand. She smiled at them, but as one started to speak Clifton slipped through the group to her side. "Go get your shower," he ordered, and walked with her to the clubhouse. "What happened to you in the first two games?"

"I didn't concentrate enough," she answered.

"You played as if you thought you had it in the bag, and then when she made a monkey out of you, you played up-tight."

She didn't want to admit this. She didn't know it had been obvious. Maybe it wasn't to anyone but him, who knew her game so well. She hoped not.

"If I'm right," he went on, "you'd better take my advice. Don't underestimate anyone."

"I know. I won't." She wished he would say something nice about the rest of the match, but he didn't. She guessed he didn't want her to forget those first two games. There was more to learn from what had happened in them than from all the advice anyone could give.

While Clifton waited for Vicky on the clubhouse porch Aunt Nan joined him, and presently John Bartlett came up the broad steps toward them. With him was a man in his thirties, mahogany tanned, trim as an athlete. Bartlett introduced Jack Kiley and explained, "Jack is Northern California representative of the Banner Sporting Goods Company. They make Vicky's racket. He'd like to talk to you, Mr. Clifton."

Kiley bowed to Aunt Nan and shook hands vigorously with Clifton. "This is a pleasure." His teeth shone starch white in an ingratiating smile. "I watched your daughter's match. She's unbelievable for a thirteen-year-old."

Clifton proudly nodded. "She's good," he admitted without a trace of diffidence.

"Too good for the juniors," Kiley stated, and promptly added, "I gather she likes her racket."

"Seems to," Clifton agreed.

"We'd like to have the specifications and see she's kept supplied."

"She's got two," Clifton told him, wondering what condition was attached to this offer.

"She ought to have six—a player of her caliber. With that powerhouse drive of hers she could easily break a string in two rackets in a match," Kiley pointed out. "We'd string them with sixteen-gauge gut. It doesn't last long, but it's fast."

"She's used to what she's got," Clifton said. "I don't want her to change now."

"I don't mean now," Kiley said in quick agreement. "After the tournament's over, it won't take more than a couple of sets to get used to it, and it'll add fifteen to her speed."

Clifton looked to Bartlett for confirmation, and Bartlett nodded. "It will. Attacking the way she does, she wants to get the ball off as quickly as she can, hurry her opponent."

"All right, then, and thank you," Clifton smiled, but asked at once, "What'll that come to?"

"What do you mean?" Kiley's eyebrows arched.

"How much will it cost? Four more rackets with that kind of gut in them? I can give you a check now."

Kiley laughed. "I don't think you understand. We don't want you to pay for them."

"But I want to," Clifton insisted.

"Out of the question. We have a list of players as long as your arm that we give rackets to. It's part of our promotion.

We're proud to have Vicky use our racket. You might say she's doing us a favor."

"This is all new to me," Clifton admitted. "But you must expect something of her in return."

Kiley shook his head. "Just to win."

Vicky came to the porch from the locker room in a boat-necked dress of light brown linen, tightly belted around her small waist. In the strong midday sun, her skin had almost the sheen and tone of the fabric. Warm color still tinted her cheeks, softly as a watercolor wash. Her eyes, clear and intensely green, held no expression of her victory as she looked about for her father.

Kiley was first to see her. He nudged Clifton. "There's Vicky. She's looking for you. She doesn't seem very excited about winning."

Clifton looked around, called to her. "She shouldn't. She hasn't won the tournament yet."

"She will, the way she's playing, and she'll be a lovely-looking champion."

"Thanks." Clifton hadn't thought much about Vicky's looks. He'd been too preoccupied with her game and her temperament to notice how her strong features had fined down in the last year. Had they been more delicate, they would have been her mother's. And her figure was taking on a shapeliness he hadn't noticed, either: the curve of her hips, the soft swelling of her breasts. She was beginning to look adolescent. She'll have to start wearing a bra soon, he thought, and then, with a nostalgic sadness, added to himself, She's not a child anymore.

He could see what Kiley meant, and he realized that the tomboy image was a thing of the past. He took her hand when she came to his side, introduced her to Kiley, and told her of his offer.

"That's wonderful!" Vicky exclaimed.

"We're delighted you like our racket." Kiley gave her his warmest smile and thought that if the spectators were ever allowed to see the animation that shone in her face at this moment, she would have an enthusiastic and devoted following rather than the impersonal admiration for workmanlike skill and precision that he sensed motivated their interest now. "Will you let me have one of your rackets?" he requested. "I'll take the specifications in the pro's shop and give it back to you in a little while."

"Oh, yes. I'll get it." Vicky dashed back to the locker room. Just inside the door she stopped abruptly at the sound of her name.

"Clifton bugs me. Never says a word to you on the court. She goes on playing like a machine, never missing anything. I hope you beat her, Gloria."

Vicky recognized Polly Perkin's voice. She didn't want to hear what they were saying about her, and she didn't want to go in there and get the rackets she had left on the bench. It would embarrass her as much as them if they knew she had heard them. Gloria Colt, defending her title, was the player she would meet in the final if they both won their semi-final matches. Evidently Polly thought that was a foregone conclusion.

"Got any ideas?" Gloria asked.

"For one thing, you're taller than I am. She won't lob you as easily as she did me."

"Big deal! What I mean is—has she got *any* weakness?"

There was a short silence. "Maybe you'll find one somewhere. I couldn't. I hope you get the breaks. She might blow if she starts losing a few points—you know, net cords and stuff like that. So far, no one's pushed her. Just don't let her scare you."

"She's only thirteen. It's crazy."

"I know."

The shower door banged shut and the conversation stopped. Vicky trod noisily into the locker room.

Polly gave her a brief, embarrassed glance, muttered "Hi" and averted her eyes. Then, quickly, she left the room. Vicky picked up her rackets and followed her out. Her father had gotten his way. They were afraid of her. She smiled to herself. That would make it all the easier to win.

She didn't repeat to her father or Aunt Nan the conversation she had heard, but she didn't forget it, and when she played seventeen-year-old Mary Morris in the semi-finals the following afternoon, Vicky was certain, as she piled up game after game, that she saw signs of fear in her older and taller opponent's faltering spirit. Mary had to be capable of better tennis to get this far in the tournament, but now she was unable to prolong a rally for more than three or four shots, and seemed to find Vicky's service almost impossible to handle. One first service knocked the racket out of her hand and she picked it up with a shrug of hopelessness.

The gallery sat mesmerized, as Vicky attacked the ball from every position with blazing force and pinpoint accuracy, and only when the end came did they engulf her in a torrent of applause. She had lost eight points on her own errors in two love sets.

Outside the court, pressing reporters blocked her way before Clifton could get to her from the stands. The substance of the questions was the same: what did she think had made her so good at such a young age?

"My father," she answered unhesitatingly.

"I didn't know he played tennis, too," one said, surprised.

"He doesn't," she told him.

"Well, what do you mean?"

Vicky realized, then, that her father wouldn't want her to answer that question; that, in any case, there was no simple answer to it. Instead, she replied, "Jerry Potter has helped me a lot, too."

Over their heads she saw her father's looming figure and sent him an appealing glance. Clifton cut through them to Vicky's side. "Go get your shower," he ordered, and at the reporters' protests he explained, "I don't want her to stiffen up. I'll answer any of your questions that I can."

They were not pleased, but Richard Cox of the *San Francisco News* spoke up. "She gave you the credit for her success." When Clifton shook his head, he went on, "I've been doing my homework on young champions, and I keep coming up with Suzanne Lenglen as the greatest—won the world's hardcourt championship at fifteen. They all say her father was her Svengali—"

"I know nothing about that," Clifton retorted, tight-lipped.

"Well, what is it you do for her," Cox pursued.

"I tell her what I know about competition, competitive temperament. Period. She's a good worker, and she's a natural athlete. That's why she's good."

"Lots of these kids work hard—"

"They may not have the spark," Clifton ventured.

"Would you say she has the 'killer-instinct'?" Ben Ryan, of the Oakland *Star*, suggested.

"Looks like it," Clifton said. "But you fellows have seen her play. Draw your own conclusions." He left them and went to the porch to wait for Vicky.

9 When they got home in the late afternoon, the phone was ringing. Aunt Nan hurried to the living room to answer it, and they heard her say, "Why hello, Eddie. Yes, she's here. We just walked in the door." She put the phone into Vicky's outstretched hand.

"I thought you'd come to the match," Vicky opened with a rush, although she hadn't, until this minute, wondered why he hadn't come.

"I couldn't get a ride," he said. "But I'm coming tomorrow. My father's taking me."

She gave an exasperated little sigh. "You could have gone with us. Why didn't you ask?"

"I didn't want to bother you."

"Oh, Eddie—how stupid can you get!"

"Your father wouldn't like it. The paper said something about him . . ."

"What paper!"

"The *News*. Don't you read them?" he asked, incredulous. "The stuff about your matches?"

"Dad won't let me till the tournament's over. But what did the *News* say?"

The phone was taken suddenly from her hand, and Clifton spoke to Eddie in, he hoped, a genial voice. "You'll have to excuse me for butting in like this, Eddie, but I'd rather you didn't discuss the newspaper stories with Vicky. They're all here for her to read when the tournament's over. There's a stack a yard high waiting for her."

"Sure, I understand." Embarrassment was clear in Eddie's voice. He couldn't tell Clifton that what he had been about to divulge didn't concern Vicky, but her dictatorial parent, and that the story contained a quote from John Bartlett to the effect that Clifton maintained he could make a national women's champion of his daughter in two years and that this probably explained the discipline that isolated her from other players and the press.

"I really phoned to congratulate her for winning her semi-final," Eddie said instead. "And my father and mother said to congratulate her for them, too."

"Thank you very much, Eddie. We appreciate that. Here's Vicky again." He handed the phone back to her.

"I'll see you tomorrow," she said shortly. "Thanks for calling." She hung up and turned on her father who had taken the evening papers to the sofa and spread them on his lap. "Read what it says and tell me please," she cried.

"Our agreement still holds," he told her and turned to the sports pages of the *News*.

"It says something about you," she went on insistently. I want to know."

"Drop it," he ordered. "You can read it all when we get home tomorrow."

"But it upsets me not to know," she said, voice rising.

He raised his eyes quickly. "Don't try that on me, Vicky. I know what I'm doing."

"Come on, dear, help me prepare dinner," Aunt Nan said and drew her into the kitchen with her. "I've read all the papers except this evening's," she told her in a conspiratorial whisper. "They say very nice things about your game, but I know what your father means. He wants you to concentrate on what you're doing, not what anyone says about it."

"I wasn't thinking about me. I was thinking about what they said of him."

Aunt Nan put a bunch of carrots on the counter and handed her a paring knife. "Fix these for me, please."

Vicky took up the knife and began to scrape the carrots. "Maybe they're bugged because he came to my rescue."

Aunt Nan, who had no wish to pursue the subject, was nevertheless curious. "What do you mean?"

"Those reporters, asking all those questions when I came off the court. Dad got me out of it. He told me to go take a shower, and they didn't look as if they liked it."

Aunt Nan gave a last shaping pat to the meat loaf and put it in the oven. "They're doing their job the same as you are, Vicky. Remember that when you talk to them. You're certainly not afraid of anything they'll ask, are you?" As she spoke, she began to grease the potatoes for baking.

"I'm not afraid of anything," Vicky asserted. "It's the kind of questions they ask—I blurt out things—"

"What sort of things?"

"I don't know. I don't want them to get the idea that Dad does all my thinking for me."

"What he advises you to do, he understands best. He's never tried to tell you how to play, has he?"

Vicky shook her head.

"When you're older and have had more experience, you can make your own decisions about everything you do. That's part of growing up."

"How much older?"

"A good deal. Slice the carrots thinner, will you, dear?" Aunt Nan had no real conviction that she was right. Frank was far too fond of his role as mentor, she thought, ever to let go of the reins entirely. And with this belief, one of the tennis articles she had read during the week disturbed her. It was an account from England of the forthcoming first Open tournament at Wimbledon, where the amateur world championships had always been held, and it was the general opinion, the reporter wrote, that the professionals would dominate. Only a handful of amateurs were of recognizable class. This meant that tennis had become a way of life, a business, for the great majority of players.

There was nothing wrong with this, Aunt Nan felt, except that whenever money entered the picture it usually meant dog-eat-dog, and eventually, she had no doubt, Vicky would become involved in it. She could foretell Frank's reasoning: financial security, making a fortune out of pleasure; turning a skill to a logical, profitable end. And this might happen sooner than she thought. If Vicky won the women's national title when Frank predicted, she would still be in high school. He would, no doubt, argue that she could play in the important tournaments and do justice to her schooling. But plans for her education included college, and Aunt Nan imagined this would be dropped if Vicky had the opportunity to travel all over the world.

She wished she knew what Eleanor would have had to say about all this. Perhaps she *did* know, and that was what troubled her. She could almost hear Eleanor saying, "All things in their time." I'm rushing the gun, Aunt Nan thought. Vicky hasn't won her first tournament yet. All the same, it was hard to imagine that she wouldn't, or that the thorny decisions weren't lying around the next bend in her path.

10 Vicky felt the same secret nervousness that she had before all her matches, the clammy palms and cold, twitching stomach. But she knew, as she had after her first match, that these familiar symptoms of keen tension would disappear as soon as she hit the first ball in the warm-up.

It was a glorious day for tennis—warm, clear sky, windless. Above the club on the grounds of the long, balconied Claremont Hotel, the palm trees were motionless.

The stands around the number one court were already filled, although it was twenty minutes before her match—the first of the afternoon. Boxholders were strolling toward their seats. She didn't know why Aunt Nan and her father preferred to sit in the stands when they had been offered seats in Mr. Bartlett's box unless they felt nervous, too, and didn't want to talk to anyone. She supposed it was much harder on the watchers than the players when they had their hearts set on someone's winning.

She hurried up the steps and into the locker room, heard a babble of voices and then, in the short hallway, Gloria passed her, followed, Indian file, by her supporters and advisors, like a little court. Gloria spoke briefly to Vicky—the Queen addressing the Crown Princess—and swept out the door.

Vicky went into the dressing room, closed the door behind her and got leisurely into her tennis clothes. In an hour, she thought, I'll be back in here taking a shower, and I'll be the champion.

With her coltish legs and skinny figure and high-pitched voice, Gloria reminded Vicky of Jeanette McGraw. This was unfortunate for Gloria, for Vicky decided to pretend that she was playing Jeanette instead of Bob, as she usually did, and unleash all the animosity she had felt for Jeanette since the accident on the roof.

In the first few minutes of the match, Vicky knew exactly what Gloria's friends had told her to do. Play short and lob. For even though Vicky had grown an inch in the last six months, it had only brought her to five feet five, so her reach wasn't very long. But Gloria and her friends hadn't calculated Vicky's pace and depth, and Gloria couldn't control the ball against them. Her short shots fell near the service line instead of the net, presenting Vicky with "set-ups," and her lobs, not high enough, deep enough, nor disguised, were easily brought down in winning smashes.

And then Vicky played short shots and lobs of her own, but with skill and deception, and Gloria pantingly pursued them until Vicky could hear her heavy breathing on the other side of the court. Gloria leaned on her racket, face flushed like a sunset, narrow chest heaving, and Vicky knew it was almost over. She allowed herself the luxury of blasting the ball from corner to corner in the sheer delight of hitting as hard as she could, without bothering with finesse or a change of pace. Forcing Gloria far out of court on one side, she would pass her down the other before the panting girl could get within reach of the ball. The end was obviously a relief to her.

Vicky hadn't counted her own errors that gave Gloria the points she won, but she thought there hadn't been more than a half-dozen, and they hadn't added up to a game.

Jeanette was forgotten when they shook hands at the net. Vicky felt rather sorry for Gloria when the runner-up cup was presented to her. She looked so wistful—the dethroned champion. And then she put Gloria, too, out of her mind and wondered what came next. Unaccountably, she thought of Chris who had really given her her backhand. How would she have done against the woman champion today? She couldn't imagine, now, Chris's making any shot or using any strategy to which she, Vicky, didn't have the answer. And then she thought, It will come soon—a test against her in a tournament. Much sooner than I expected. For she knew that she wouldn't stay long in the junior ranks. Not after today.

There was no restraint in the gallery's applause now. The six games Vicky had lost in the first three rounds were all she lost in the tournament and the spectators knew they had been watching greatness. There were many among them who had seen it before, but they couldn't recall such devastating superiority as they had seen today. Of course, this was only the juniors, but Vicky so far surpassed the field that they could think of her in terms of women's tennis and imagine what another year's experience would do for her game. She played like a boy and yet she had the grace of a ballet dancer, and she had the canniness of a born competitor. If she always seemed to be where the ball was, it was anticipation, not guesswork, that telegraphed the shot. Only the strength and endurance of a youngster, pitted against those of a woman, might falter, but Vicky's resourcefulness might not let it come to such a test. So the gallery acknowledged her as great without reservation, their applause still thundering as the press photographers took their pictures of the cup presentation, of the girls shaking hands again, of Vicky alone.

And then Vicky was in the dressing room again, looking at herself in the long mirror. "You did it," she whispered to the image.

As Vicky left the locker room to join her father and Aunt Nan on the porch, she saw Kathryn Gates and Roger Halloran coming across the lawn toward the clubhouse. Behind them Eddie, alone, waved to her. She had an instant impulse to retreat, back to the locker room where they couldn't follow her, but her feet were rooted where she stood, and then they were in front of her, smiling.

"Congratulations!" Kathryn cried. "You were groovy!"

"You sure were. How does it feel to be champ?" Roger asked.

Vicky wanted to laugh. They sought her out now. At school they had avoided her. She kept her face expressionless. In a small, cold voice, she replied, "It doesn't feel like anything."

Undaunted, Kathryn went on, "I read about all your matches. You only lost six games in the whole tournament. I didn't know you could play like that." Her eyes were bright with awe.

"I didn't either," Roger said.

"Thanks," Vicky told them in a voice as expressionless as her face, and she went to the edge of the steps to call Eddie.

Slack-jawed, Kathryn and Roger stared at each other. Color was rising in Kathryn's face and when she found her voice it was shrill. "What a swellhead!"

"Creep," Roger muttered. "Come on. Let's watch the boys' final."

They passed Eddie on the steps and he said "Hi" to them but they went on without answering. "What's with them?" he asked Vicky.

"They want to be friends now that I've won. They make me sick."

Eddie saw the blaze in her eyes, recognized the warning signal, but he hazarded, "Maybe they're sorry for the way they acted, Vicky, and they're really glad you won—"

Anger stiffened her back and drew hot color to her cheeks. "Are you on their side?"

"Cool it! You know I'm not." He smiled at her stormy face. "I just think you could be nice about it now. And you'd better be careful. You might get your picture taken looking like this," he teased, hoping to cajole her.

She threw a quick, nervous glance around the porch. "You're a kook. There're no photographers here."

"I know. But there could be. Now you're the champ, they'll take your picture every chance they get." He looked at her with affection. "You were great. Everyone's saying so. The people around me in the stands were saying they never saw anyone like you. You know what one man said?"

"What?" she asked.

"He said, 'It's ridiculous for her to be playing these kids. She ought to be playing the women.' "

Vicky was pleased. That was what she thought, too.

"And it's true," Eddie added. "They can't even give you a game."

"Vicky!" Clifton's voice boomed the length of the porch.

She took Eddie's hand. "Come on," she urged, and pulled him after her.

"Gentlemen," Clifton said to a group around him when

the two came over, "this young man here, Eddie Marsh, started my daughter playing tennis—spent hours practicing with her. What did you think of her today, Eddie?"

Eddie felt a lump the size of a lemon in his throat. He hadn't expected any credit. "I was just a bangboard for her," he said.

"You started her really working. That's the important thing," one of the men said, and then Clifton introduced him to Vicky and Eddie. He was Harlan Brooks, a round little man with a round, ruddy face and a thatch of white hair—and he was president of the Northern California Tennis Association. "We have plans for you, Vicky," he said.

She wanted to know immediately what they were, but her father was introducing the others to Eddie—John Bartlett and Bob Carter, whom he remembered, and who said they remembered him well; Jerry Potter and Mike Wilson and Howard Welsh, the president of the club who had presented the trophies.

Finally, as the torrent of talk ebbed, Aunt Nan said, "Tell her, Frank."

Clifton, clearly in the flush of full vindication, nodded. "Vicky, Mr. Brooks was telling me the association wants to send you to the national juniors in Philadelphia."

"Oh!" Vicky was delighted. "When?"

"In August."

"That's terrific!" Eddie cried, and gave her hand an impulsive squeeze.

"And after the juniors," Bartlett said, "we want you to go on to New York and have a look at the National Open. If you win in Philadelphia, you'll probably be playing at Forest Hills next year."

As Vicky cried her delight, Aunt Nan drew in her breath

inaudibly. Pushing, pushing. They weren't even letting her grow up. Good Lord, she'd only be fourteen. Why didn't they leave her in the juniors a couple of years, let her win without pressure.

Phillip Marsh stood on the lawn, shading his eyes, looking the length of the porch for his son. When Eddie saw him, he excused himself and ran down the steps to him. Pointing to the group where Vicky stood, he took his father's arm and pulled him forward. Marsh shook his head and drew back.

Vicky watched Eddie, saw Mr. Marsh's reluctance to join them, and nudged her father. "There's Eddie's dad. I want you to meet him."

Clifton went to the railing and called out, "Mr. Marsh, come on up here."

"I want to watch the rest of the boy's final," Bartlett said. "I'll be in touch with your father about your trip, Vicky."

The others, taking their cue from him, congratulated her again, said goodbye to Aunt Nan, and followed Bartlett to the court.

Vicky didn't remember that Mr. Marsh was shy, and just for an instant, she wondered if what she had done today had anything to do with it. Thinking back, she recalled that the people who had pressed forward for her autograph after the match had seemed to look at her with a kind of curiosity and awe as if she were no longer the girl who had entered the tournament. It must be something the reporters had written, she thought, and was glad that she could read all the newspapers tonight and see what they had said about her. It didn't occur to her that the magic of her racket on this day had produced such an effect.

Clifton and Aunt Nan thanked Mr. Marsh for all the help Eddie had given her. The thin little man seemed to warm at that, but he disclaimed any credit for his son. "The credit's all hers," he said seriously. "I felt as if I were watching a ballet dancer with the power of a pile driver—if that makes any sense."

Clifton laughed. "I know what you mean."

Marsh's eyes, pale blue in the strong afternoon light, were fixed steadily on Vicky. "One wouldn't think, to look at you, that you could hit the ball as hard as you do," he observed, taking in her slender figure.

"It's a lot in timing," Vicky explained. "That's one of the things Eddie helped me with."

Eddie looked pleased but embarrassed, and Clifton gave him a pat on the shoulder. "We know what he did, and we're grateful."

"I'm sure Vicky can break training now," Marsh said with a half-questioning inflection. "I wonder if you will give Mrs. Marsh and Eddie and me the pleasure of having you all for dinner at the Mark Hopkins tonight?"

"The Top of the Mark!" Vicky's eyes widened with delight. She had never been to a hotel for dinner. She turned bright pleading eyes to her father and Aunt Nan. "Can we?"

"I think it's a great idea," Clifton said appreciatively to Marsh, "but let it be my party."

"Wouldn't think of it," Marsh refused. "Shall we say seven o'clock?"

"All right, Nan?" Clifton asked his sister.

"Yes, indeed. It's very kind of you, Mr. Marsh," Aunt Nan agreed, and mentally ran through Vicky's wardrobe, finding it lacking in a suitable dress for this occasion.

Eddie grinned happily at Vicky. He was really going to be part of her first big victory, and he was thinking what a great guy his father was to make it possible.

It was midafternoon when they drove away from the club and Aunt Nan, sitting in the front seat beside her brother, said, "Head for Oakland, Frank."

"What for? It's out of the way."

"I want to give Vicky a present for winning—a new dress for tonight. We can get something nice at Magnin's, and it'll be easier to do it here than in the San Francisco store."

"Oh, Aunt Nan!" Vicky cried from the back seat. "Can I have black?"

"No, darling. Anything but black. You'll have years to wear that."

"She'll need things to go with it—shoes and a purse. Get those for me," Clifton said, sorry that he hadn't been first to think of getting her a present.

"That'll be neat, Dad! I'm sure glad I won the tournament."

Clifton looked at her face in the rearview mirror. It was glowing as she looked down at the silver trophy close beside her on the seat. He hoped the fringe benefits of winning would never mean more to her than the game. They could become very tempting in the future. They could make a new dress look like a bagatelle. He, like Aunt Nan, was aware of the new tennis professionalism and the emphasis on money; but, unlike her, he had in mind a careful course for Vicky in that direction.

It was five o'clock when they got home with Vicky's new clothes. She put the trophy on the window seat where it shone in reflected sunlight, and picked up the evening paper Clifton had bought on the way. She took it to the sofa and flipped the pages quickly to the sports section. There it was—her name on the first page in a banner headline and in the center her picture, smashing an overhead. She was several feet off the ground, one balancing leg outthrust, as she made the shot. It was a graceful, dramatic stroke the photographer had caught and she looked at it admiringly before she began to read the column to the left. Then her eyes flew down the lines of print: "Completely outclassing the field, thirteen-year-old Vicky Clifton won the Pacific Coast junior title at the Berkeley Tennis Club today, defeating the defending champion, Gloria Colt, 6–o, 6–o in the final, and losing just six games in the tournament. The youngest player ever to win the title, Vicky's extraordinary power and command of every stroke made her opponent look like a novice. Old-timers were comparing her with Suzanne Lenglen, who won the women's hardcourt championship of France at the same age and went on to become the greatest woman player in the world.

"Shortly after the final, a spokesman for the Northern California Tennis Association announced that Vicky will be sent to Philadelphia in August for the national junior tournament.

"Gloria, four years Vicky's senior, fought all the way in a hopeless effort . . ."

Vicky suddenly heard her aunt's voice calling her to the phone. When she picked it up, Aunt Nan said, "It sounds like a young boy." Vicky was aware that her aunt and father were listening when she said "Hello" and heard the piping voice reply, "This is Tony." Her hand suddenly felt cold and clammy on the phone, and a strange constriction seemed to paralyze her throat. She swallowed, and managed to answer in a small voice, "Oh, hello, Tony." Her eyes turned wide and fearful on her aunt, whose own stiff features and compressed lips gave her little comfort.

"I'm glad you won the tournament. I read about it in the paper. You sure clobbered her."

"Thank you , Tony," Vicky said with relief. "It's awfully nice of you to call." Behind her, she heard her father's long sigh.

"What kind of a cup did you win?" Tony went on. "Is it silver?"

"Yes. Would you like to see it?"

"Yes," Tony cried, delightedly.

"I'll bring it down now to show you." She didn't know what she had expected Tony to say when he called, but it certainly wasn't this. She would have hugged him if he had been there at this moment, so grateful was she that he no longer hated her, that he was glad she had won, and that he wanted to see her—well, see the cup, anyway.

She put down the phone and picked up the trophy. "Tony wants to see my cup," she announced excitedly and started for the door.

"Just a minute." Clifton's voice stopped her halfway across the room. "We have to be at the hotel at seven, and you have to dress. You can show it to him tomorrow."

"He wants to see it now." Their eyes met and held, steady and unyielding. Vicky's mouth tightened in a hard, straight line.

"Let her go, Frank," Aunt Nan spoke up. There was no sense in spoiling this day with a test of wills. But more importantly, she knew what it meant to Vicky to close the breach with Tony. Frank should know that, too. To Vicky she said, "Be back no later than six."

"I will," Vicky promised, and before her father could speak again, she was out of the apartment.

She felt that all eyes must be on her as she ran down the hill to the grocery store, her cup tucked under her arm. It was like a banner, she thought, proclaiming "best junior on the Pacific Coast," and her arm squeezed gently on it.

At the foot of the hill, she turned into the doorway beside the grocery store and rang the Mercatis' bell. Instantly, the buzzer sounded and she pushed open the door. Tony must have been watching for her. She climbed the flight of stairs to the flat on the second floor. A door opened a crack and then Tony flung it wide, his mouth hovering on the brink of a smile.

"Hello," Vicky said nervously.

"Hi," he said, and slowly grinned. His eyes, so large and dark, looked pleased. "Come in." He stepped aside.

She walked into the small, square living room and stood in the middle of it on a mustard and green patterned rug. Tony invited her to be seated on the brown mohair sofa placed across the two windows on the street side, and he perched on the edge of a matching upholstered armchair. The room was drab but tidy. Even the shaft of sunlight, filtering through lace curtains, was unable to lift the gloom from dark furniture, dark wallpaper, and brown-framed pictures of dreary landscapes.

For a moment there was silence between them, broken only by the loud ticking of a clock in the dining room beyond.

"Here it is," she said abruptly, and thrust out the cup.

"Hey!" Tony exclaimed and jumped up to take the trophy. Slowly he read the inscription, turned the cup around to examine it. "This is neat."

She saw again the scar on his left wrist and noticed the stiffness of it and the unnatural backward bend of the hand as his fingers turned the cup. With a quick surge of guilt she looked away from it. Her only comfort was that he had jumped up from his chair and when he had come to her to take the cup his step was light, no longer clumsy as it had been at school.

"How did you beat her so easy?" he asked. Shining eyes rose from the cup to question her, then returned to the inscription. " 'Pacific Coast Championship—Girls' Singles—1968—Winner.' You have to have your name put on, don't you?" he went on before she could answer his first question.

She nodded. "I guess they do it at the store it came from."

"The paper says you're going to the national junior tournament." He handed her the cup and went back to his chair.

"In August," she replied matter-of-factly, thinking how funny it was that she could hear it mentioned and speak of it as calmly as if it were a trip across the bay. Perhaps it didn't seem so exciting now because she was sitting here seeing Tony's deformed hand, knowing that he could never do the thing he liked best. While she was becoming a famous tennis player, he might have become a famous violinist if it hadn't been for that awful day on the roof.

"Do you think you can win?" he questioned.

"I hope so," she answered. "I guess it depends on how I play on grass."

"Grass!" Tony echoed.

"In the East they play all the big tournaments on grass," she told him. "Tennis started on grass."

"That's crazy," he said. "How can the ball bounce on that stuff?"

"I don't know. But it does," she answered.

"Tell me about your game today," he asked, and his face lit up again, like that of a small boy wanting to be read to.

She settled back against the hard sofa, trying to think of some way to make it sound exciting to him.

The front door opened, and Mrs. Mercati stood on the threshold, staring unbelievingly at her, then at Tony, and back at her. She had a round face, round dark eyes like her son and, at the moment, a florid complexion as surprise turned to anger. She closed the door noisily and came into the room. "Why are you here?" She threw the question, in a harsh tone, at Vicky, who stood up politely. Tony sprang from his chair and cried, "She brought her cup for me to see, Mama."

Mrs. Mercati's eyes moved to the silver trophy. "To rub in how good you play tennis with your good hands?"

Her words, razor-sharp, stung Vicky. "Tony said he wanted to see it," she informed Mrs. Mercati, and clamped her mouth shut.

"I did!" Tony confirmed. "I phoned her and I told her I wanted to see her cup." His pleading, embarrassed glance was lost on his mother.

"He was nice," Vicky told her defiantly. "He congratulated me, and *I* asked him if he wanted to see—" she began . . .

"I don't want to hear," Mrs. Mercati interrupted, and Vicky moved past her to the door.

Tony went after her, and at the doorway grabbed her arm. "I'm sorry," he apologized softly.

"That's all right, Tony." She opened the door. "I guess your mother has a right to be mad at me." She gave him a half-hearted smile and wished he'd take his hand from her arm so she could go.

In a whisper he asked, "Would you teach me how to play tennis? I wouldn't tell her."

Vicky's smile widened. "Yes, I would!" she whispered back. "Just as soon as I get home from the nationals." She left him grinning happily. Before he closed the door, she heard Mrs. Mercati yell, "What were you talking about?" and she knew that Tony would think of something to tell her.

Her father and Aunt Nan were dressing when she returned. She went quickly to her own room, grateful that she didn't have to answer any questions right now about her visit. While she dressed, she could figure how to avoid telling them what Mrs. Mercati had said, without lying. As for teaching Tony how to play tennis, she had plenty of time to figure out where and when she could do that. She'd rather not think of what her father would have to say about it if he knew.

"Was Tony pleased to see your cup?" Aunt Nan asked when they had gathered in the living room, ready to leave. Vicky thought she really wanted to ask, "Was he pleased to see *you?* Has he forgiven you?" but there was no hint of it in her casual tone and mildly curious expression. And Vicky answered, equally casually, "He sure was."

"Was Mrs. Mercati there?" Clifton asked.

"Oh, just before I left," Vicky said and quickly changed the subject. "How do you like my dress, Dad?" She stood still before him, shining bronze hair and skin almost of a color, eyes and the green of her new dress nearly matching.

"Very, very nice," Clifton said approvingly. "And the girl in it's very pretty. Come on, now. We've got to get going."

Vicky thought Eddie looked almost handsome and much older than fifteen in his dark suit and white shirt. She had never seen him dressed up like this before. For a moment she imagined his red hair black, his freckles gone, his shoulders broader, and then she felt disloyal, for he was looking at her with open admiration and surprise. He liked her as she was.

Following the maitre d'hotel, they all threaded their way between tables to one reserved by a window. Vicky noticed several glances of recognition from other diners, and was glad that she looked nice—that they all did, especially Aunt Nan, whom her father sometimes called Duchess when she was dressed for a party.

The music began, and Marsh said to Vicky and Eddie, "I guess you two would have preferred a place where they play rock all the time."

"Oh, no," Vicky replied promptly and politely. "I like it here," and she looked through the broad expanse of window across the room to the distant, dimming mass of the Marin County hills. Lights were beginning to sparkle like yellow diamonds on the hillsides and along the waterfront. "I like the music, too. It's nice."

"You want to dance?" Eddie asked.

Vicky got up. She didn't know how they would dance to this kind of music. She hoped she wouldn't step on his feet. But Eddie danced very well, and she followed him easily. It was fun dancing like this, for a change. Close in his arms, she smiled up at him.

"You're so pretty when you smile," he told her. "Why don't you ever smile on the court?"

"Why should I?" she asked.

"You win so easy, you ought to look like you're enjoying it." He gave her a teasing look, but his criticism disturbed her and she put her cheek to his so she wouldn't have to look at him. "Don't you enjoy it?"

"After it's over." She felt herself stiffen and missed a

step. "Anyway, I'd look silly going around the court smiling all the time."

"I don't mean all the time," he protested. "I mean like when your opponent makes a good shot and wins a point. It doesn't happen very often. You wouldn't have to smile much."

"I'm concentrating when I'm playing."

She felt his shoulder shrug beneath her hand. "Someone sitting behind me today called you 'Little Stone Face.' I wanted to knock his block off. I knew you were concentrating. You never smiled when we practiced, either. But now you're a champ, I think—"

"Let's dance and quit yakking." She felt anger well up in her, now. He didn't have to tell her that and spoil her evening. She wondered if the people who had recognized her tonight were thinking—even saying—"There's 'Little Stone Face.'"

Her face grew hot against his. She stepped on his foot and muttered an embarrassed apology. He was making her clumsy. "Let's sit down," she said, and when they went back to the table, she knew that Aunt Nan saw in her expression that something was wrong. The others didn't seem to notice. They were too busy talking. She wished she could go home.

But of course she couldn't for hours yet. She just hoped Eddie wouldn't ask her to dance again, even though he was looking at her now with sheepish, apologetic eyes as he held out her chair for her. He sat down beside her, stiff and silent, and unfolded his napkin on his knees.

"We ordered for you," Marsh said. "Hope you like filet mignon."

"Who wouldn't?" Eddie said.

Vicky, deep in thought, didn't speak. Clifton repeated

Mr. Marsh's question rather sharply. "You want steak, don't you?"

"Oh, yes. That's fine." She gave them all a forced little smile, and caught Aunt Nan's quick, curious glance.

"Your father tells me you're going to Oregon on a fishing trip next month," Clifton said to Eddie.

"We camp out—it's great. Last summer . . ." From the enthusiasm of his reply and the eagerness with which he launched into a description of last year's trip, Vicky knew he was as relieved as she was that he didn't have to make conversation with her.

The music stopped. Crab cocktails were served and Vicky ate hers in silence until Mrs. Marsh spoke to her. "I hear you're going to Philadelphia to play. Aren't you excited?"

Vicky tried to look as if she were. "Yes. I think it's wonderful. I didn't expect it."

"Philadelphia's my home town," Mrs. Marsh said. "I've been telling your father of a delightful inn not too far from the club."

"Oh, tell me about the club!" Vicky leaned toward her, her interest genuine now.

When the music began again, Vicky thought, I won't dance. I'll say I'm tired. I'll say anything.

But as the others got up to dance, it appeared Eddie wasn't going to suggest it. Left alone, they sat staring at the lights thickly sprinkled now on the Marin hills, at the people across the room, at everything but each other. And the music seemed to go on interminably.

Finally Eddie said contritely, "I didn't mean to upset you."

"Why did you then!" she flared.

"I thought if you knew, you might—"

"I won't. I won't do anything different than I do."

He saw the flush spreading over her cheeks and resolved to say nothing more. Maybe if they called her "Little Stone Face" in the papers—but they wouldn't. They admired her concentration. They called her "imperturbable as a summer sea."

For Vicky the evening began to drag again. She danced with Mr. Marsh and then with her father. As he led her smoothly around the floor, she said, "When can we go home, Dad?"

"Aren't you having fun?" He gave her a look of surprise. "I'm tired."

"Oh, I'm sorry, dear. We'll sit down. We can go home before long."

A short while after they returned to the table, he said to the Marshes, "I think we'd better take our girl home. She's had a lot of excitement today and she's feeling tired."

"I should think she would," Mrs. Marsh said understandingly.

Aunt Nan said nothing until they were in the car and on their way. "What was the matter with you tonight?" she demanded then.

Clifton frowned at her. "What do you mean, Nan?"

"Vicky knows what I mean."

"Nothing," Vicky said. "I'm tired, that's all."

"Tell me the truth." Aunt Nan swung around to face her in the back seat.

Vicky was silent until Clifton, too, demanded, "Well, what was it, Vicky? Speak up."

"It was something Eddie said," Vicky admitted.

They waited for her to go on, and she saw it was useless to hedge. If they didn't get it out of her now, they would later. "He said someone in the gallery called me 'Little Stone Face.' "

Clifton laughed. "Good Lord, is that all!"

"It's enough," Vicky blurted.

"Since the subject's come up, I think you could look a little less—well—you could smile once in a while," Aunt Nan ventured.

"Like a damned Cheshire cat?" Clifton protested.

"No. As if she's enjoying the game."

That's just what Eddie said, Vicky thought.

"She's not out there to have fun. She's out there to win," Clifton stated heatedly.

"Oh, Frank!" Aunt Nan shook her head and turned back to stare unseeing out the windshield. What was he doing to Vicky? she wondered. Where would it lead?

The weeks following the tournament sped by. Leaving Vicky to Jerry's training, Clifton spent long hours putting his business affairs in order to turn over to his assistant, Mark Robbins, while he was away. Vicky practiced with renewed incentive, taking her lessons from Jerry and playing sets with Bob and Mike, and was pleased that the matter of her attitude didn't come up. She had half expected it might after what Eddie and Aunt Nan had said, and at first, she was so conscious of her unchanging expression that her concentration suffered, and she found herself playing mechanically, undeceptively. Then she thought to herself, I may not turn on a smile when my opponent makes a good shot, but I don't glower either. If Jerry or Bob or Mike thought she was a little stone face, they'd say something about it, politely she was sure. They understood. Aunt Nan couldn't, and Eddie should. Finally she put it out of her mind and concentrated on the shots Jerry thought needed polishing: the sharp crosscourt forehand and backhand and the backhand smash.

Aunt Nan went about her business of getting Vicky's

clothes in order for the trip—new things she would need, others drycleaned and laundered—as if her niece were going to be gone two months instead of two weeks. When Vicky didn't have time to go shopping with her, she brought home clothes for her to choose from. New luggage was delivered, and everything to be packed was put by itself in a large hall closet and checked off on the list she had made.

Two days before Vicky was to leave, Jack Kiley sent her six new rackets with zipper covers. Aunt Nan noticed that these seemed to please her more than the new clothes. Perhaps they're symbolic, she told herself. The equipment of a champion. She wondered if six changes of tennis clothes and shoes were enough.

11 The morning of departure arrived—a clear, warm Wednesday. At the airport, Aunt Nan seemed very subdued, and faint worry lines around her eyes surprised Vicky. "I wish you were coming with us," she said, and gave her a fierce hug, suspecting Aunt Nan was upset because this was the first time they had been separated since her mother had died.

Aunt Nan patted her arm and forced herself to smile. "I'd be a bundle of nerves," she confessed. "I haven't gotten used to your tournament playing yet." It was true. If it weren't such a *business*, she would have enjoyed it. But there was Frank to consider, too. He wanted Vicky to himself without interference, without suggestions. There would come a day, she thought, when her opinion would count for something; when the dehumanizing of Frank's competitive psychology would hit a snag.

The flight was called. Vicky's heart missed a beat, and she felt for a moment as if she were flying to the ends of the earth.

"Write to me when you have a chance," Aunt Nan said. She was still smiling, but she seemed to want to get the leave-taking over with. She took their arms and walked with them to the gate. Clifton bent down and, kissing her cheek, found it hot.

"Take care, Nan," he said. "If you need anything, call Mark Robbins at the office."

She nodded and then watched them disappear into the plane.

As the plane sped eastward—or the land sped west, for the plane seemed motionless in the sky—the fertile farmlands of the Missouri and Mississippi rivers seemed to breathe with a gentle rhythm beneath them. The great rivers lay like snakes sunning themselves in the shimmering midwestern day.

And then the industrial lands usurped the earth, with smoke stacks replacing mountain peaks, and crowded cities in place of the quiet open stretches of the farms.

After five hours, the order to fasten safety belts flashed on, and the plane began its gradual descent to Philadelphia.

They were met at the airport by a bustling young woman, dark-haired, slender, mini-skirted, who introduced herself as Mary Tucker from the Philadelphia Cricket Club and said, with a pleasant little laugh, that she was the official welcoming committee.

Determined to be helpful, she took their luggage tickets, and when she had retrieved their suitcases and the rackets, she got a porter to carry them to the entrance. Clifton and Vicky followed in her wake, Clifton with an amused smile. He hadn't expected this sort of reception, nor was he used to young women doing his legwork for him.

"It's kind of you to take all this trouble," he said to her, and noticed that she was rather pretty with fair skin, silken black hair, and shining dark eyes.

"No trouble at all," she answered. "If you will wait here, I'll get my car." She took off in long strides toward the parking area.

Clifton tipped the porter before she could try to do that too.

"She's nice," Vicky said, as impressed with their reception as her father was. "I guess we can ask her to get me a game in the morning."

"Later, Vicky. Let her catch her breath."

Driving away from the airport, Mary Tucker said, in a business-like voice, "Your association asked us to make reservations for you at the Crystal Brook Inn. I got you connecting rooms on the back. I thought it would be quieter."

"Fine," Clifton said.

"You'll like the inn. It's attractive and the food's good. And Vicky—you don't mind if I call you that, do you?"

"Oh, no," Vicky hurriedly replied.

"—I've arranged practice for you tomorrow morning with one of our best women players."

Vicky opened her mouth to speak, but her father said, "Vicky only practices with men or good boy players."

"But Mrs. Walsh is *very* good—"

"I'm sure she is. Do you have a pro?" Clifton asked.

"Yes, of course." She paused. "Mrs. Walsh will be so disappointed. So will the others."

"What others?" Clifton asked, shifting his legs to ease the cramp in one calf. These bucket seats shoved up against the dashboard weren't meant for the likes of him.

"The other ladies I lined up to practice with Vicky." She looked at Vicky in the rearview mirror. "We've read all about you, you know."

"You did? Back here?"

"Yes. You're news. There was an article about you in the *Enquirer*—being the youngest player to win a major tournament. We're all dying to see you play. You'll probably have a gallery when you practice—"

"Oh, no," Vicky cried.

"She doesn't mean a real gallery," Clifton quickly told Vicky, whose reaction gave him a qualm. People watching her practice had never seemed to make the slightest impression on her before.

"Heavens—you're used to that, aren't you?" Mary's frown was half surprise, half annoyance. She was beginning to wonder if they had a young prima donna on their hands.

"Yes, but—" Vicky sensed a warning in the stiffening of her father's back. "I've got to get used to grass courts. I'll probably be terrible until I do," she ended lamely.

"Spectators won't bother her," Clifton said to Mary. He didn't want her or anyone else to get the idea that Vicky was a nervous player.

Vicky leaned back in her seat and watched the lush countryside roll by.

"Have you ever been east before?" Mary asked, changing the subject.

"I have but Vicky hasn't," Clifton answered.

"I imagine you'll want to do some sightseeing."

"Yes, we'll find time for that. But not too much. She's got to conserve her energy. She's not used to the heat and humidity you have here."

"I guess you plan her routine carefully." Mary's tone held a slight barb, Clifton thought, as if she realized now that he ran interference for Vicky, laid the ground rules, kept his daughter's mind on the business at hand.

"I do," he answered simply.

"I hope it isn't so strict you can't have dinner with my family and me tonight."

Clifton felt as if she were pushing him into a box. She ought to know that Vicky needed rest after the trip and the excitement of the day without forcing him to make the excuse. More coolly than he intended he answered, "Thank you. Not tonight, if you'll excuse us. Any other—except Sunday—"

"Of course. We'll fix another time, tomorrow." She fell silent. Clifton had a feeling the subject wouldn't come up again, which was just as well. They weren't here to socialize, and he knew dining with strangers would be a strain on Vicky. He wanted her to have every break, to make the adjustment to unfamiliar surroundings and courts as easily as possible. Alone with her, without diversions, he could keep her schedule as it had been in California, both for practice and for her matches: go to the club just in time for her to dress leisurely, and when her practice or her match was over, leave. No hanging around yakking with people, no fraternizing with the players. Early dinner and to bed by nine. That was the way it had to be.

"About the pro," Clifton said. "Would it be possible to arrange practice for Vicky with him?"

"I'll call him first thing in the morning and let you know. He won't be at the club now."

When they drew up before the two-story fieldstone inn in Chestnut Hill, Mary blew the horn for the porter and got out to open the trunk.

"Dad, you sounded grumpy," Vicky whispered to her father.

"I did?" Clifton said, surprised. "I didn't mean to. I'm sorry." He got out of the car and held the seat forward for her to squeeze out from the back. He could tell that he had embarrassed her.

Mary came around the car to them as a porter came out

to take the luggage. "I'll call you at nine in the morning. Will that be too early?"

Clifton gave her a warm, appreciative smile. "No, that will be fine."

"And I'll pick you up," she told him.

"That's very kind of you, Miss Tucker," Clifton said, aware of Vicky's eyes on him, "but I arranged to rent a car before we left California."

"I see," she said. "Well, that *will* be more convenient for you."

Clifton put out his hand to her. "Thank you for all your trouble."

"Thanks a lot," Vicky added, and noticed that Miss Tucker's smile was thin, her glance at her father appraising.

"Not at all," Mary said. As she drove off, the tires skidded with a protesting squeak on the graveled driveway.

"*She's* mad," Vicky said.

"Don't be silly," her father said lightly, and they followed the porter into the inn.

Their rooms, connected by a bath, overlooked a small stream that meandered across a corner of the wooded grounds. Through the open windows, Vicky could clearly hear it running over its rocky bed and tumbling into a pool before continuing on its way down a hidden slope. Flower gardens rampant with summer blooms bordered the inn and encircled a velvet green lawn dotted with garden furniture. A few chairs were occupied by guests chatting over after-dinner coffee or drinks in the pastel afterglow.

Looking down at the garden, Vicky felt herself relax, as the tension of the drive from the airport sloughed off. From the bathroom, she heard the buzz of her father's electric razor, and presently he called out, "Are you getting ready for dinner, Vicky?"

She turned from the window. "I will when you're through in there." She opened her suitcases and hung up her clothes, noticing that Aunt Nan had packed them so carefully with layers of tissue paper that there wasn't a wrinkle in any of them. She chose a French-blue linen dress with a round neck and buttons down the front and laid it across the bed. She had a different dress for every day of the week, and three "dressy ones for parties, just in case" as Aunt Nan had described them. But Vicky wondered if she would ever have a chance to wear them.

"All clear," her father called, and she heard him go into his room and close his door to the bathroom.

She felt a cloud of unhappiness drift over her again as she slipped out of her clothes to take a shower. Things wouldn't be any different here than they were at home, as far as making friends and having fun were concerned. Aunt Nan had just hoped they would be, and so, she realized, had she. Still, she had to admit the only reason she was here was to win the tournament. Maybe she'd feel better again when she'd had something to eat. It seemed a long time since she'd had lunch somewhere over the Missouri River.

Even though it was nearing eight o'clock, the dining room was filled, and others, like themselves, were just arriving. At a bar piano in a far corner a young man was softly playing popular show tunes. The guests were well-dressed, and predominantly in their twenties to early middle age. Vicky was the only teen-ager in the room.

The headwaiter led them to a small table at the side of the room and presently a waiter took their order. Vicky looked around her, eyes wide and bright. This wasn't like it was at home before a tournament. There they had dinner at six-thirty and she was in bed by nine; here they wouldn't finish dinner before nine. But she knew it wouldn't be like this every night.

Clifton saw her pleasure and blessed Mrs. Marsh for having recommended the Crystal Brook. This unavoidable late-dining one night wouldn't matter. He'd have Vicky back on her training schedule tomorrow. In the meantime, let her enjoy it. They could even sit out under the stars for a while after dinner.

Vicky was gazing at a table near a garden window. The object of her interest was a young man with a party of six, whose animated gray eyes in a mahogany tanned face were fixed on the young woman opposite him. He appeared to be twenty-one or -two. The young woman said something to make him laugh, and he threw back his blond head and displayed a row of very white teeth above a square, jutting chin.

Clifton noticed that Vicky was looking at the young man with open fascination and that she seemed, at this moment, no longer thirteen years old. The unwitting stranger had stirred depths in her that Clifton neither anticipated nor welcomed at this stage of the game.

He was somewhat relieved when the waiter served the first course, and Vicky turned her attention to her food. But between courses her eyes kept straying to the young man, and she replied in monosyllables to the conversation her father tried to make. They were just finishing their entree when the party of six rose to leave. Vicky watched the young man walk across the room to the entrance, his tall figure and massive shoulders towering over his friends.

When they had disappeared through the doorway, Clifton smiled softly at his daughter. "Now will you talk to me?" he asked.

12 After the first flurry of embarrassment at her father's knowing smile, Vicky tried to behave as if she had never set eyes on the young man in the dining room, and the ensuing rush of talk about the trip, about grass courts, about anything that popped into her head amused Clifton, but it worried him a little, too. She was over-excited and he wanted her to have a good night's sleep. Perhaps if he got her back on the tennis track and kept her there.

"I've been thinking about the pro, Vicky," he said. "He may make suggestions to you about your game. He may think it's his job to do it if the grass bothers you. Whatever he says, don't make any change in your grips. Tilden says the ball takes a low, skidding bounce off grass—"

"I know, Dad. I've thought of it," she said. "I'll have to quicken my timing, that's all."

"Your footing may not be as secure as it is on hard courts."

"I don't know about that. I'll have to see. But don't worry. I'll work it out," she assured him.

"Let's sit outside for a while," he suggested. "Then you'd better get to bed."

"I'm not tired," she said.

"The sack will feel pretty good to you. To me, too."

Later it did, and she was soon asleep. Once in her dreams

she was at the Top of the Mark and the orchestra was playing rock. Dancing opposite her, gray eyes laughing into hers, was a young man in Eddie's dark suit. His hair was blond, curling about his ears, his skin deeply tanned. "They call you 'Little Stone Face'," he shouted above the music, and all sound stopped while his words echoed through the room. She awoke with a start and sat up in bed. She put her hand to her heart, expecting to feel it pounding as it had in her dream, but she couldn't even feel its beat.

"Don't be crazy," she admonished herself. "He doesn't know you're alive." She dropped back on her pillow, but it took her some time to fall asleep again.

From the start, Vicky felt that grass was her game. The softness under foot was a delight after hard courts, and although the eleven o'clock sun was strong, there was no deflected heat from the surface. All her strokes, particularly her serve, seemed more effective—hanging low, taking the long, skidding bounce of which Tilden wrote; all except the drop shot that died on the turf with more finality than on hard courts. So effective was her serve, she felt as if she had more time to get to the net behind it even though the pro, Ben Jones, took the ball on the rise.

Her father was clearly surprised and pleased. Standing off to the side, in line with the net post, he was able to see the increased and punishing speed of her shots and the attitude of confidence with which she made every stroke. She hadn't even found trouble in adjusting her timing to the fast ball. In fact she seemed to revel in the quickened pace of the game, and when the first set ended as the heat of midday was becoming more oppressive, Clifton heard the pro say, as they paused at the net before changing sides, "I don't see how anyone in this tournament is going to stop you." He had won the first set 6–4, but he had had to work for it, and only his superior reach and length of stride had made the difference. "Feel like another?" he asked. "Not too hot for you?"

"I always play two practice sets." She toweled off and wiped her racket handle.

"I meant you don't want to overdo it until you get used to the humidity," he explained. Thin as a reed, the nut-brown man with sun-bleached crew-cut hair and bulging right forearm seemed scarcely affected by the heat or by the running Vicky had forced him to do. But Vicky was beginning to feel a pressure on her lungs and difficulty in breathing deeply.

"I'll stop if I get tired," she said.

As they began the second set, several club members sauntered over to the court from the clubhouse porch, and soon they were playing before a small gallery. Clifton wished that Mary Tucker were among the spectators. He would have liked her to see why even a good woman club player couldn't give Vicky much of a game. He would also have liked the chance to show himself in a more agreeable light than he had the day before.

Earlier Gwen Stuart, a large, brisk woman and the tournament chairman, had taken them in tow, shown Vicky to the locker room, and escorted them to the pro's court on the second tier beyond the long white-frame clubhouse. She had introduced them to Ben Jones and then left them, and until now Clifton had been the only spectator. There flashed through his mind the fuss Vicky had made when Mary suggested that a crowd might gather to watch her play, and he was glad to see now that she took no notice of it.

He saw, too, that she was beginning to scramble more for

the ball, that her timing was slowing down and she was bending rather than stooping to the ball. While she still kept the speed on her service, she was slower in getting to the net and Ben was passing her easily. Clifton could hear her panting and was not surprised when, at o–4, she held up her hand and said, "I think I'd better stop."

The pro nodded agreement and the small crowd dispersed. Clifton wanted to yell after them, "That's not her game. Don't spread it around that she's slow and has no stamina." Then he thought, with some satisfaction, They'll be in for a shock on Monday. The optimistic part of his mind believed this, the cautious part asked if he expected too much of a thirteen-year-old in this climate. It was the one condition he hadn't taken into account in his ambitious timetable for her achievements.

"I was terrible," Vicky groaned, and wondered if she could possibly get used to the damp, smothering heat before the tournament began.

"You'll shape up," Ben encouraged, and gave her a pat on the shoulder. "You'll learn to conserve your energy— walk more slowly between points, don't chase impossible shots."

"I didn't think I'd mind the heat." She held her towel to her face and felt her pulse hammering in her temples.

"It's different than your California heat," he said. "It's more tiring to go for low shots. You've got three days before the tournament. You'll get used to it. Would you like to play tomorrow at the same time?"

"Thank you. I would."

"Do you think she ought to do some running?" Clifton asked.

"I think her practice is enough for her," Ben advised, "with the humidity as high it is." He paused. "Just don't worry about it. Take it in stages."

"We might do a little sightseeing," Clifton proposed.

"That's a good idea. Get her mind off tennis," Ben approved.

One thing encouraged Vicky. After her shower she felt thoroughly refreshed, without a trace of fatigue, and she realized that it wasn't her body that had let her down in the second set; it was the struggle to breathe. She would try what Mr. Jones had suggested, although it wouldn't be easy to let "impossible shots" go. She was too used to playing every point as if it were the last one.

On the way to the inn for lunch, Clifton tried to keep his concern out of his voice. "I want you to keep in mind that there's nothing wrong with your endurance. It's a matter of controlling your breathing the way you control your timing. And you've got to realize that you were excited your first day on grass, in a strange place, preparing for a big tournament. You've broken that ice now."

"I felt as if I'd run out of gas," Vicky told him. "But I felt fine after I had my shower."

"You're going to be all right," Clifton said, reassuring himself as well as his daughter. But each knew the other was worried.

After lunch they went sightseeing, but Vicky found that nothing took her mind off her game—not even Independence Hall or the Liberty Bell, and when they had seen them she was glad that her father suggested going back to the inn.

They had six-thirty dinner in the dining room along with a few children and elderly guests. There was no music, and Vicky knew she would not see the blond young man, but she didn't care. She felt a compulsion to get this day over with and get back on the court tomorrow.

Standing at the end of the clubhouse porch waiting for

Vicky to dress for tennis, Clifton felt an apprehension he couldn't shake. Endurance in this muggy heat was the one thing he could not have prepared her for in California, and there wasn't time enough now to do it. Somehow, she would have to figure a way to combat it, doing what the pro suggested and anything else that might help—like a handkerchief soaked in cold water around her neck, he suddenly thought. Preoccupied with his concern, he started when Mary came up behind him and called his name. He swung around, and at sight of her, his somber expression dissolved in a smile. Lord, she's pretty, he thought in the moment before he said, "Hello, there."

Her hair, that had fallen to shoulder length the day before, was now drawn back and tied at her neck with a filmy lime-green scarf the color of the dress she wore, and her face, tilted up at him, bore no sign of displeasure, he was happy to see. When he had met her, he had judged her to be in her early thirties. Today, she scarcely looked as if she were out of her twenties.

"How did it go yesterday?" she asked.

"Quite well," he answered, excusing himself for the white lie. "We like your pro. Vicky's playing with him again this morning."

"Oh, good. I was afraid she'd finished. Do you mind if I watch?"

"Certainly not." Then he added as a kind of insurance against her misjudgment of Vicky's game, should the heat affect it again, "She had a little trouble with the humidity yesterday—"

"Do you wonder? It was in the high eighties."

"It didn't get to her until the second set. I think she'll get used to it by Monday." I hope, he thought.

"I don't think you can get used to it," she said, sensibly. "You just learn how to cope with it."

"That's right. Mr. Jones gave her a couple of pointers that ought to help."

"At least all the girls will have the same problem if this keeps up," she reminded him. "How does she like grass?"

"It seems to suit her game very well," Clifton said.

Vicky joined them, and Clifton thought she was as pleased to be greeted by Mary's friendly smile as he had been. Walking with them across the springy turf to the pro's court, Mary said, "Mother would like you for dinner tomorrow night."

Clifton caught the warning in Vicky's quick glance, but whether it was against acceptance or refusal he couldn't tell. "We'd love to," he accepted. "What time?"

"Would seven be all right? You can leave as soon after as you like. We're not far from the inn—just about ten minutes."

"Thank you very much," Vicky said and Clifton knew that she, too, was relieved that amends were made.

A small boy who had just finished his lesson passed them as they approached the pro's court. He gave Vicky a curious, owlish look and a tentative smile before he ran on.

"Gwen Stuart tells me the kids are quite excited about seeing you," Mary said to her. And glancing over her shoulder at the small figure, Vicky noticed a group of young players on the porch staring in her direction. "Gwen told them not to bother you," Mary added quickly. "They won't come barging over here."

"I wouldn't mind it now," Vicky said with embarrassment.

"You know how it is the first day on strange courts," Clifton put in. "It's like football practice when you're trying out a new formation."

Mary looked up at him, with interest. "Did you play football?"

"He was All-American," Vicky informed her proudly.

Mary's smile flashed at him. "You and my father will certainly hit it off. He played at Amherst."

"What do you know!" Clifton smiled in return. "I look forward to meeting him." But his real and instant pleasure was in knowing that something about himself interested Mary.

The pro tossed the last of several dozen worn practice balls into a basket and came across the court to meet them. "Morning," he said; then to Vicky, "How do you feel?"

"Fine," she replied. She put her towel on the net post and started onto the court. Ben followed her. "I want you to try something," he told her, and that was all Clifton heard as he and Mary sat down on the turf a short distance from the sideline.

"Do you know what pacing yourself means?" Ben asked.

"I don't think so."

"It's like budgeting your stamina so that you have enough left for the final stage of a match. Say you've been attacking, rushing the net, going for everything, and suddenly you're winded, you really feel bushed. Change pace for a few points. Play from the backcourt. Keep the ball deep and well-placed, but don't try to hit the cover off it. If your opponent goes to the net, lob high and deep. If he smashes one you can't get, don't waste your strength trying to run it down. Then when you've got your second wind, you can go all out again."

Vicky frowned. "I don't know if I can do that. It sounds like playing pat-ball, and like not trying. I like to win every point I can."

Ben shook his head. "You've got it wrong. It's smart tennis. You don't let down mentally. You simply slow up the game. Often it takes the sting out of your opponent's shots—throws him off as well as giving you a breather. I've seen the best of them do it in long matches. You may not have to do it in the juniors, but when you get up against the top women, it'll be useful to be able to do it—especially in this kind of heat."

Vicky nodded, but she was still unconvinced. That wasn't her idea of match play. Give her opponent no quarter; run her into the ground: that was her kind of game. But how about yesterday? She couldn't have run anybody into the ground in that second set. The pounding in her ears, the ache in her lungs, the rubbery feeling in her legs—she didn't want that again.

"I'm going to play you as hard as I can," Ben told her. "If you get tired, try it out. And remember what I told you yesterday about walking slower between points."

"I don't want to look like I'm stalling," Vicky protested.

"You won't."

"All right," Vicky agreed. "If I get tired." But I won't, she thought. I won't.

It seemed as if Ben played every point to tire her. When she went to the net, he lobbed, sending her racing to the backcourt for the ball; and when she returned it, he drop-shotted, forcing her to scurry up. He crisscrossed the court with sharply angled shots, but having forced her wide to the sideline, didn't hit into her open court for a winner. Instead, he hit a shot she could get, to keep her running. She had never played against anyone with his control and thought that he had played only as hard as he had to to beat her the day before.

All that her skill and power had earned her was just one game to his five. She stood still for a moment on the baseline before serving. She could hear her heart pounding, feel it thudding against her rib cage. She took a deep breath, held it for a second, then hit a serve wide to his forehand, foregoing her powerful first service and staying back. When he returned the ball to her forehand corner and came to the net, she lobbed to his backhand corner. As he ran back to retrieve it, she had time, she realized, to breathe slowly and deeply and felt the beat of her heart decreasing. The lob bounced out of his reach. She moved slowly to the left court to serve, this time a high-bouncing top-spin shot to his backhand. He returned it to her backhand corner, starting a driving duel that tested her anticipation. This instinctive quality, coupled with the first lesson she had learned—never take your eyes off the ball—brought her into position to hit without rushing. Even though it went against the grain for her to drive with top-spin instead of pummeling the ball, she hit the less demanding shot.

Following his advice, she had taken the sting out of *his* game, and was at 4–5 when she suddenly struck out again, resuming her swift pace, flat service and net attack. She got to 6–5 before he put on a burst of pressure and ran out the set at 7–5.

Although she could feel the sun like a hot iron against her flesh, and perspiration plastered her shirt to her back, she breathed without any more effort than if she were jogging around the block. Confident that Ben had given her the answer to playing in this heat, she knew she would never again be panicky as she had the first day. Perhaps, too, she was getting used to the climate, and she had learned how to breathe. She smiled to herself. "Like learning how to breathe underwater."

There was no let-up in her speed, net game, or effort in the second set, and Vicky knew, at the end of it, that she would be ready for the tournament. Even though Ben had won the set 6–3, she had no complaints about her tennis or her stamina. Nor did Ben.

"That's more like it," he said and looked pleased that his advice had proved valuable. He put a damp arm across her shoulder as they walked over to join Clifton and Mary. "How did you like that?" he asked them as they got up from the grass.

"I can't believe it," Mary said. "Thirteen! I think the women had better look to their laurels."

"That was good, Vicky," Clifton said with such obvious relief and pride that Vicky knew how much better than "good" she had been. She wished she were playing in the national women's next week instead of next year.

13

The Tuckers' house stood on a low hill against a backdrop of trees. It was an oblong, fieldstone house of impressive proportion. Two chimneys pointed stubby fingers at the watercolor sky. The house threw out a warm and welcoming aura like a friend standing at a gate with open arms. To right and left of a wide lawn, white plank fences squared two fields, and in one of them horses grazed lazily.

The long driveway that took Vicky and Clifton to the house swept straight up the hill and circled around the entrance.

"Gee!" The word burst from Vicky. Her eyes swept the wide face of the house, but settled on the horses. "They must be very rich, Dad."

"Probably are," he answered.

"I wish we were rich."

He gave her a narrowed, sidelong glance. "What would you like that you haven't got?"

"Horses," she said.

"Come on," he laughed. "You've never ridden a horse in your life."

"I would if I had one. I'd be a good rider."

"I daresay." She would be good at anything that interested her, he thought, as long as it involved action, competition, proving herself the best. Lord grant she wouldn't lose interest in tennis until he'd seen her to the top.

"Do I really look all right?" she asked, and smoothed the skirt of her favorite green dress.

"You know you do."

"Do I look older than thirteen?"

"What do you want to look older for?"

"So I won't be treated like a kid."

"You look older than a kid," he assured her, and swung the car around the circle to the broad stone steps.

The door was opened by a maid in starched white cap and apron over a dark green uniform. "Good evening," she said, and held the door wide as they stepped into a large, square hall.

"Good evening," Clifton responded. "I'm Mr. Clifton—"

"Yes, sir. This way, please."

He and Vicky followed her to a large living room, half-shadowed, half-bright with the setting sun's reflected light. Matching sofas flanked a high, wide fireplace at one end of the room. On a table against a side wall, a massive arrangement of roses faintly perfumed the room. In front of a sofa against the opposite wall was a coffee table, and on it was a large crystal bowl of white asters.

Mary was coming toward them with that long, gliding stride of hers. "Hello," she said, smiling a warm welcome. "Vicky, how pretty you look."

"Thank you," Vicky murmured with unusual shyness.

Clifton wanted to say, "And how lovely *you* look," but Mr. and Mrs. Tucker were on Mary's heels, greeting them, and Mrs. Tucker was saying, "We're *so* glad you could come." She put out a hand to Clifton and felt it disappear in his. She was about Mary's height and size, with Mary's warm coloring, but not pretty like her daughter. Her features were too sharp. Her eyes had an inquisitive squint. But her cordiality belied the sharpness of her face. Tucker shook hands with Clifton and the two men moved off, talking.

Mrs. Tucker turned to Vicky. "And this lovely young girl is the tennis champion." Her glance swept Vicky from head to foot. "You don't look big enough to hit the ball as hard as they say you do."

"They're not all brawny, Mother," Mary laughed.

Mrs. Tucker took Vicky's arm. "Come over here and sit down beside me. I want to hear all about you." She led Vicky to the sofa against the wall, facing open French doors and the sweep of lawn. "Mary tells me you're an absolute genius."

"Oh, I'm not," Vicky demurred, managing for the first time to get in a word.

Mary sat down in an armchair beside the sofa. "Well, I've never seen anyone like you at your age. You should have seen her serve, Mother. Just like a boy."

Vicky looked over at her father and saw that, as Mary had predicted, he and Mr. Tucker were "hitting it off." A tray on a stand held bottles of every shape and size and Mr. Tucker, busily fixing drinks, was laughing at something her father had said. Presently, he brought drinks in squat glasses to Mrs. Tucker and Mary and ginger ale to Vicky.

Vicky wanted to get off the subject of tennis and herself, and when Mrs. Tucker and Mary were sipping their drinks, she said, "I saw your horses in the field."

"Do you ride, Vicky?" Mary asked.

"No, but I'd like to."

"When the tournament's over, you must come and ride with me before you leave. One of the horses is very quiet and gentle. You could ride him."

"Old Twister. Of course you could," Mrs. Tucker agreed.

"That's a funny name for a horse," Vicky said.

Mary explained. "When he was younger, I used to hunt him. He had a habit of twisting over jumps. I don't suppose they foxhunt where you live."

"No, they don't."

"You hunt with a pack of hounds. The hounds chase the fox and you follow the hounds on horseback."

"That must be exciting."

"It is. But you have to be a very good rider to do it."

"What about the jumping?" Vicky asked.

"You jump fences, stone walls—"

"Wow!" Vicky cried softly, remembering the height of the fences around the fields. "Do you do that here?"

"No, but you and I would ride here. I could lend you some clothes."

"I'll ask my father." Vicky's excitement began to abate. She could imagine her father answering, "Are you crazy?"

She looked over at him again. Mr. Tucker was talking to him, and her father was staring at a small, silver-framed photograph he held. His brow was slightly knit as if something about it troubled him, and then he put it down on the table between them. She couldn't see it very clearly, but it looked like a photograph of someone in uniform.

"What do you do besides play tennis, Vicky?" Mrs. Tucker asked.

"Nothing, except go to school."

"I should think it would be good for you to have another interest. You really must come ride with Mary. The young friend we've asked tonight to meet you—she's playing in the tournament, too—rides here quite often."

"Who is that?" Vicky asked abruptly.

"Ellen Basker," Mrs. Tucker answered. "Have you heard of her?"

"No, I haven't."

"She's the Pennsylvania State junior champion," Mary told her. "We thought you'd like each other. She's older than you. This is her last year in the juniors, but you both will have a lot to talk about, I'm sure."

"I guess so." Vicky tried to look pleased. But she wished they hadn't asked Ellen to come. She had thought she would enjoy this evening, but now she felt herself going stiff and guarded.

At that moment she heard a doorbell ring faintly and saw the maid cross the hall, and then they were in the room— Ellen Basker and behind her, towering over her, the blond young man in a canary yellow jacket.

Vicky's mouth went dry, and she felt tiny beads of moisture gather on the palms of her hands. She pressed them surreptitiously to the edge of the sofa.

"There you are!" Mrs. Tucker jumped up and went toward them with outstretched hands. Mary followed her and Vicky, left alone, supposed she ought to stand up, too. She did, slowly, never taking her eyes from the young man's face until he shot her a swift, expressionless glance over the top of Mrs. Tucker's head.

Mr. Tucker and Clifton stopped talking and moved toward the newly arrived guests and Mrs. Tucker introduced them. Then she brought them over to Vicky, who felt a sudden, ridiculous panic run through her—a fear that she would be inarticulate, that her excitement would show in a blush.

"Vicky, I want you to meet Ellen Basker and her brother, Julian." To them, she added, "I'm sure you've read of Vicky Clifton—"

"Of course," Ellen Basker said, smiling. "Hello."

Her brother nodded. "Hi," he said, and his smile broke warmly on her. "That was a nice article about you."

"I haven't seen it," Vicky said, surprised that her voice sounded normal.

"You must be something else." He paid her the compliment, and then looked away and said to Mrs. Tucker, "I'm sorry I have to leave, but I've got to be in Merion at eight."

"I know. I'm sorry we can't keep you here." She walked with him to the door. Vicky, deflated, watched him go. As far as she was concerned, this was the end of the evening. She had met him and he had paid her a compliment—well, sort of. He didn't say she *was* something else. He thought she was just a kid—a kid who was a tennis champion. So what?

She sat down again, dejected, on the sofa. Ellen dropped down in the corner of it and faced her, her long, brown legs crossed. Her straight blond hair fell to her shoulders and framed a plain, round face. She had none of her brother's good looks, Vicky thought. Her eyes were a friendly, dull brown, her nose too short.

"What's it like, playing in California?" Ellen asked her.

"What do you mean?"

"I mean, on those courts? Are they very fast?"

"Depends," Vicky said, "whether they're asphalt or cement."

"It must be nice to play outside all winter."

"Sometimes it's quite cold," Vicky said, trying to look interested.

"Do you play sets or just practice shots?"

"Both." Vicky thought she was going to start getting technical now.

"Will you practice with me tomorrow?" Ellen asked.

"I'm playing with the pro," Vicky answered. It wouldn't be necessary to tell her that she never practiced with girls, and she was glad she didn't have to sound rude. As a precaution, she added, "I'm playing with the pro every day until the tournament."

"Oh," Ellen said.

The announcement for dinner broke up the tennis conversation and when they were seated at the table—Vicky and Ellen on one side, opposite her father and Mary, and Mr. and Mrs. Tucker at the ends—Vicky seized the opportunity to steer Ellen onto the subject of her brother.

"Does your brother play tennis?" she asked casually.

"No, he's a golf nut."

"He's very good," Mr. Tucker put in. "Plays on the Princeton team, doesn't he, Ellen?"

"He did," Ellen said. "But he flunked math and Father made him quit until he passed."

"He's studying to be an architect, like his father," Mr. Tucker told Vicky. "He's a junior now, isn't he, Ellen?"

"He will be when he gets back."

Vicky made a quick calculation. She would be fourteen this fall, and he was either nineteen or twenty. No wonder he wasn't interested in her, even if she didn't look thirteen. But maybe, if he got to know her, if she could make friends with Ellen . . . but the trained part of her mind rejected friendship. Ellen was a possible opponent. At the moment, though, her father wouldn't notice whether she was making friends with Ellen or not. He was too interested in talking to Mary, leaning toward her when he spoke. Vicky saw it and then looked away as if she had been prying, and wondered how soon after dinner they could leave.

When the time finally came to go, Vicky forgot to ask her father about riding until Mary reminded her as they stood in the doorway, and then she asked, offhandedly, "May I come over and ride with Mary after the tournament?"

"What! Good Lord, no!" Clifton cried with consternation. "I mean, it's very kind of you, Mary, but she doesn't know the first thing about riding. I can't let her take the chance of hurting herself."

Mary looked more disappointed than Vicky. "I understand. I'm sure she wouldn't get hurt, but I guess you're right."

Vicky's silence as they started for the inn was heavy with discontent and Clifton thought he knew what was the matter with her. It wasn't unusual for a kid her age to have a crush on an older boy. But this was ridiculous. She had only seen him twice and hadn't spoken more than a few words to him. As soon as the tournament got under way, she'd forget everything else. He just wished she could conceal her feelings as well off the court as she did on it.

"You like Mary, don't you?" she asked suddenly, startling him.

"Of course I do. Don't you?" He gave her a sidelong, wary glance.

"Sure." Then she added, "Do you think she's as pretty as Mother was?"

"Oh, come off it, Vicky." His tone was impatient, but he felt his heart beating like a schoolboy's, and there was a certain apprehension in it. He'd have to watch his step. He hadn't realized he had been so obvious. "No one's as pretty as your mother," he added with total sincerity.

"I don't think so, either," she said.

"Mary was engaged to a very handsome fellow," he went on, as if that would change the picture. "Her father showed me a photograph of him. He went through a year's fighting in Vietnam and the first day after he got home he was killed in a car accident on the Pennsylvania Turnpike."

"That's terrible. When did it happen?"

"A couple of years ago."

Vicky thought about it. She remembered the expression on her father's face as he looked at the picture. How long did it take anyone to get over something as horrible as that? She guessed her father was wondering, too.

Later, when Vicky was in bed, Clifton sat by his window smoking, his thoughts in a jumble. He was far from free to think straight about Mary. He had Vicky to consider, first and foremost. They had a job to perform together, and it was his obligation, since she was prepared to do her part of it, to keep her from worrying about anything. It had never occurred to him that this situation with Mary would arise. He wasn't even sure it *was* a situation, for it took two to make one; and other than being charming and seemingly interested in everything he said to her, he couldn't put his finger on a single expression in her face or voice to match his infatuation.

He stubbed out his cigarette and began to undress. For the first time, he wished Nan were here. Her very presence would keep him on a single track. She would be a constant reminder that he had yet to prove to her the wisdom of the decision that had brought Vicky here.

14 Vicky looked at the tournament draw late Monday morning on her way to the locker room to dress for her first match. Ellen was in the upper half with her, but in the lower quarter. They couldn't meet before the semi-final. The champion and defender, Nancy Gilmore, was in the lower half. Vicky looked no further. Except for the southern Californians, the names meant nothing to her, anyway.

Clifton did not look at the draw at all, and it would have surprised him that Vicky had. He didn't hold with dissecting the draw, anticipating matches that might not take place, assuming that all the seeded players would come through as expected. Take them all as they come; play each match as if it were the final, was what he believed. Don't join the inevitable covey of complainers who moaned about their tough draw, as opposed to someone else's easy ride to the quarters or the semis. The tougher Vicky's draw, the better she would play. He was not concerned about it.

He had had only one instruction to give her, and he suspected she had already thought of it. "Go for a record. Try to win the tournament without losing any more games than you did in the Pacific Coast." He had a reason for this. He wanted her victory to be such a thumping one that there would be no question that she was ready for the women's nationals.

He gazed over the courts at the running, leaping, battling white figures and thought that half the hopes out there would be dashed before the hot morning had ended. There was an element of cruel denial in the competition: no compromise, a winner and a loser. But at least there was always another chance if the heart and the will were strong.

"Mr. Clifton?" The voice startled him, booming as it did from a large and imposing woman who had approached him from behind. He was wide-eyed and a little forbidding when he turned stiffly to her. But she went on, in her sergeant-major's voice, "I've been looking for your daughter. I'd like to talk to her. I'm Maude Bagley of the *Telegraph*."

"Vicky's dressing for her match," he told her. "She'll be glad to talk to you when it's over."

"I'll only take a few minutes of her time."

He shook his head emphatically. "I'm sorry. She never gives interviews before she plays."

"Is she nervous before her matches?" Miss Bagley inquired pointedly.

"No. Not at all," Clifton quickly denied.

At that point Vicky came from the locker room and, seeing her father talking to a stranger, went straight to Mrs. Stuart, standing at the center of the porch, to tell her she was ready for her match.

Looking over Miss Bagley's head, Clifton saw Vicky going on to the clubhouse court with her opponent. He noticed a grim set to her mouth, and two photographers who were about to record it.

"Excuse me," he said abruptly and hurried to a seat on the porch as close to the court as he could get.

Miss Bagley, following a little behind him, stored up her first impression of the young star's parent for future use.

Vicky played with a savagery that was almost embarrassing to Clifton. She so outclassed her opponent that she could have won as easily with half the effort. She went to the net behind overpowering services, simply to watch her opponent flail hopelessly at the ball. Her return of service, no less vicious, left so little margin of error that a half-dozen times she missed the lines or the corners by inches. The score, 6–0, 6–0, told only half the story. Those six errors were the only points she lost, and when she left the court, there was just a scattering of applause. The spectators couldn't bring themselves to acclaim annihilation.

Miss Bagley pounced on Vicky before her father could reach her side, but Vicky replied firmly to the reporter's second request for an interview. "I have to take a shower before I cool off."

Miss Bagley's brown eyes sharpened. "I'll wait," she said. In spite of her annoyance—or because of it—this article *had* to be written. She had reported tennis for many years, but she had never met anyone like these two—father and daughter. The girl was like a tennis robot, programmed to destroy the opposition; and the father was the programmer. Frequently, from her position beside one of the porch columns, she had looked at Clifton as he watched the match without the slightest change of sphinx-like expression, nodding from time to time. And when the match was over and he had reached his daughter at the locker room entrance, he didn't appear to be congratulating her. He spoke briefly to her, she shook her head and went into the room. He went to the end of the porch and sat down alone on one of the folding chairs.

"You gave that girl a merciless beating," Miss Bagley said later in the lounge.

"I played my best," Vicky answered, sensing the woman's disapproval.

Clifton, sitting with them, said nothing. He, too, sensed a certain antagonism in Miss Bagley, as if she regarded Vicky as a young upstart from the Pacific Coast.

"She played as if you scared the wits out of her. She's really much better than that." Miss Bagley put a cold, almost accusing eye on Vicky.

"I guess she is, if you let her play her game," Vicky said.

Miss Bagley smiled thinly. "She didn't look as if she had a game today. She hardly touched the ball." Vicky was silent, and the reporter asked, "Don't you ever give your opponent a game to make her feel better?"

"No, not ever," Vicky answered without the slightest diffidence. "I don't think they'd want that. I wouldn't."

"But you've never lost a match, have you?"

Vicky shook her head.

"I have all the background on you," Miss Bagley said. "I'd like to know more about you as a person—what do you think about when you're beating someone like that?"

For a moment Vicky gave her an impatient frown. Then she answered, "The point I'm playing."

Miss Bagley leaned forward in her chair. "I mean, do you work up a dislike for your opponent?"

"Of course not!" Vicky shot back.

"What are you trying to imply, Miss Bagley?" Clifton broke in. He wouldn't allow Vicky to be submitted to this badgering. He went on, without waiting for the answer, "To Vicky the opponent doesn't exist as a personality. She's simply a player to be defeated as quickly as possible. That's all there is to it."

"I'm trying to find out what makes Vicky Clifton tick," Miss Bagley persisted. "It's unusual for a thirteen-year-old to have the killer-instinct. Don't you agree?"

Clifton eyed her steadily, framing an answer.

"Did you instill it in her?" she asked.

Clifton realized that she had read up on him too. That's what they'd said of him when he played football. "You can't instill an instinct, Miss Bagley," he answered.

Miss Bagley ignored this. It wasn't what she had really meant. After a pause during which she seemed to scrutinize Vicky's face—her downcast eyes and compressed lips—she modified her question. "Do you think she inherited it from you?"

"I think you confuse concentration with the killer-instinct," he answered.

Miss Bagley gave him a faint smile, a smile that for some reason irritated him more than her manner or anything she said. But in a carefully modulated voice, he told her, "You will have to excuse us now. I want Vicky to have her lunch."

"I'm not quite through," she said.

"I think so." He got up from his chair. "Come on, Vicky." As they left the room, he felt Miss Bagley's eyes bore into his back. "She's bad news," he muttered.

Mary caught up with them as they were getting into the car to leave. "Vicky, you were super! I don't think you missed anything, and that poor girl—she was scared half to death."

Vicky felt almost embarrassed. "I didn't notice that. I just thought she wasn't playing very well."

"You didn't let her." Mary shifted her eyes to Clifton.

"I'm sorry I've seen so little of you both in the last few days, but I've been so busy with all the girls arriving—"

"You've been more than generous to us with your time," Clifton said, trying to look at her as if it didn't matter. "Vicky and I hope you will be free Saturday night, when it's all over, to have dinner with us—your mother and father, too, if they will give us the pleasure."

Vicky looked at him quickly, then looked with a weak smile at Mary.

"They're going to Long Island. But I'd love to," Mary accepted, and Vicky made an effort to look pleased.

"Great!" Clifton allowed his eyes to linger a moment on her face.

"By the way," she went on, "there's something I want to warn you about. I saw you talking to Maude Bagley. Be careful what you say to her."

"I had a feeling I should," Clifton told her.

"She's always out for a sensational story. She'll probe and pick for something disagreeable to hang it on, and if she can't find what she's looking for, she'll hint at something."

Clifton nodded. "I don't think I said anything she could twist, and Vicky didn't. We'll watch it, though. She's an aggressive character."

"She's more than that. She's a trouble-maker. She started a feud between two of our best young players. It was a shame. They'd been friends—"

Again Clifton nodded, but he thought, That's one thing she can't involve Vicky in.

"Of course, everyone expects that sort of thing in the rag she writes for, but it can hurt," Mary added.

"We have a rule," Clifton told her. "Vicky never reads the papers until the tournament's over. Whatever Miss Bagley writes won't have any effect on her game."

"That's a sensible rule," Mary approved. "Vicky's lucky to have you."

Clifton gave her a grateful smile. He suspected she held a minority opinion.

As they drove out of the club grounds Vicky said, "I thought we were going to Forest Hills after the tournament."

"We are," Clifton answered.

"I mean right after. Now you've asked her for dinner, we can't."

Clifton gave an exasperated sigh and swung the car from the driveway onto the road. "We have to try to repay her hospitality, Vicky."

"I don't want to hang around here after it's over." An edginess in her voice caught Clifton's ear. That wasn't all that bothered her.

"Did something unpleasant happen in the locker room before your match?"

"How did you know?" she asked, puzzled.

"You looked sort of grim when you went to the court."

"Oh." She said nothing more for several moments, and Clifton drove silently, staring at the road, waiting.

"Ellen," she said at last.

"What about her?" he questioned, surprised. They had seemed to get along well enough at the Tuckers'.

"She hardly spoke. And the others—they acted as if she had said something about me."

Clifton tried to frame the right response to this. He couldn't tell her it was her imagination. Vicky didn't imagine things like this. She never had. "There's nothing unkind she could say about you," he said. "What did you two talk about the other night? Everything was pleasant then, wasn't it?"

"She asked me to practice with her. I said I couldn't. Maybe she didn't like it."

"So—you don't practice with girls. It's a fact. If that made her mad, it's too bad." Clifton was relieved.

"And now, that Miss Bagley," Vicky went on. "She hates me and she'll write something awful about me."

He shook his head. "She doesn't hate you, Vicky. She doesn't understand you. You're very young and yet you think and play and behave on the court like someone twice your age. She can't make you out and it bugs her. That's all."

Vicky frowned. She was unconvinced.

That night, when she had gone to bed, Clifton drove out to get a *Telegraph*. The inn—it did not surprise him to learn after Mary's comment—did not carry that paper. When he had found one, he sat in the car scanning the sports pages. There was no article by Miss Bagley. A brief piece mentioned the opening of the tournament and gave the results. He gave a sigh of relief. It was foolish, he knew, to feel as if this were a reprieve, but he did. And then he realized that he had forgotten about the other evening paper. He returned to the inn, bought one and took it to his room. A three-column picture of Vicky on the second page had caught her at the finish of a backhand drive, balanced on the toes of one foot, arms outstretched. She looked as if she were in flight. "Coast Star Crushes Blake" was the caption. Beneath the picture was the story. He read it and smiled. Miss Bagley could write her venomous pen dry. It wouldn't cut much ice now.

15 It became clear as the matches progressed that the California prodigy was the drawing card of the tournament. Around whatever court she was to play on, a crowd gathered early, and Vicky and her opponent had to thread their way to it through the narrow opening the spectators made for them. The tiny explosions of photographers' flash bulbs never ceased during the warm-up, and it was often with impatience that the umpire had to request them to clear the court.

It was no longer a question among the gallery of "Will Vicky win?" but of how many games the hapless opponent would get from her. Not until she had reached the semifinal with Ellen Basker was there interest in her match as any kind of contest.

In the locker room the atmosphere seemed to Vicky to thicken with hostility as victim after victim sought consolation from her friends. In the corner she had taken for herself, Vicky accepted the brief, unfelt congratulations of a few and became accustomed to covert glances of awe and curiosity.

She had lost three games in four matches, and no match had required more than half an hour. All of Vicky's victims had the same complaint: they couldn't do anything against her net game. It was like playing against a brick wall; and she hit so hard from the backcourt that the ball almost knocked the racket out of their hands when they were able to reach it. Her anticipation was so accurate that she always seemed to be in position before the ball got to her. They were doing all the running.

The reporters, with the exception of Miss Bagley, whose piece had not yet appeared, wrote their stories. The *Enquirer* facetiously put it, "You could watch Vicky Clifton dispose of an opponent during a coffee break."

During the week Miss Bagley had maneuvered through the crowds to the courts like a ship in full sail. She had intercepted players going to and from the locker room, but she had made no attempt to speak to Clifton or to Vicky. Whatever she had wanted of them, she had evidently gotten. But when she intended to use it was a question that puzzled Clifton. Vicky seemed unaware of her; she was completely business-like, playing her matches, eager to leave the club as soon as she had showered and dressed. A couple of times he had wanted to stay for a while and talk to Mary, but Vicky had asked to leave and he couldn't do otherwise. He had laid down the routine long ago.

Only one thing troubled him. She had been too calm, ever since her second match, and he was afraid she might be getting overconfident. She wasn't interested in talking about tennis, and whether they drove through the countryside or played gin rummy before dinner or did any of the other things he contrived to fill their days, she seemed lackadaisical. The spark of excitement he usually sensed in her manner or the tone of her voice was missing. He couldn't question her about it. She was winning, and winning easily. That was all that mattered. Once he wondered if she didn't feel well, but rejected the thought. Her color was good, her eyes bright; the heat hadn't seemed to affect her at all.

And then, the night before the semi-final, she did a turn-about. She picked at her dinner, claimed she wasn't sleepy at bedtime, and asked him to take her for a walk. It was ten o'clock before he saw the slit of light from her slightly ajar door go out and midnight before he, himself, could settle down to sleep.

It was still dark when Clifton suddenly awoke with the odor of smoke in his nostrils. For a moment, wondering if he had dreamed of fire, he lay still, staring into the gloom of his room. Then, with terrifying awareness that he had not dreamed it, he sprang out of bed and went to the window. A billowing, gunmetal cloud drifted off toward the brook and a yellowish-red glow wavered on the lawn and chairs outside the dining room and kitchen at the far end of the inn. A cry of "Fire!" rang piercingly down the hallway that was coming alive with shouting voices and running footsteps. He stumbled over his shoes in his haste to get to Vicky's room, and heard a frenzied hammering on his door. "There's a fire! Get out of the building!" someone yelled.

"Yes!" he yelled back, fumbled to turn the switch on Vicky's bedside lamp, and pulled her from her bed.

"What's happening?" she cried, unsteady on her feet.

"There's a fire, Vicky. It's not in this end of the inn, but we've got to get out." He tried to speak calmly. "Put your coat and shoes on." He gave her a little shake. "Do you hear?"

She ran to the closet. Clifton got his own coat, stuffed his wallet into a pocket, slipped into his moccasins and returned to her. She stood at the door with two rackets under her arm.

Pushing through the hall to the staircase with other guests, old and young, frightened, crying children, some clutching an assortment of belongings, they could hear the muffled roar of the fire. Smoke, drifting up like a fog, stung their eyes and began to choke them. They drew their coat collars up over their nostrils and started down the stairs, buffeted, then separated by the crush of bodies converging from both ends of the hall on the central escape.

In the lobby, Clifton tried to reach out for Vicky, but he was swept along through the thick and acrid smoke and the hot glow of the fire on the right. Someone was trying to direct them. "Keep calm, please! Don't crowd the door!" The warning shout was scarcely heard. The heavy body of a woman pressed Vicky against the jamb of the door. She felt her racket heads dig into her breast before her father's arms enveloped her and together they pitched out onto the porch. Sucking the air in gulps, they ran blindly across the lawn, until their cooling skin told them they were safe. When they looked back at the fire, the yellow-tipped flames were lashing through the shattered windows, licking the blackened fieldstone walls upward toward the roof. Through the crackling and roaring, there was a sound like a distant explosion. A shower of sparks fell over the dining room and the floor above erupted in flames.

They heard the sirens then, wailing along the road. Fire trucks screeched through the pillared entrance and fanned out before the building. Behind them, an ambulance drew up on the lawn. Helmeted figures with hoses, chemical apparatus swarmed from the trucks. Ladders swung up to the height of the inn.

Clifton felt his arm, tight around Vicky's shoulder, tremble. "God, I hope everyone got out," he prayed. Vicky pressed closer to him and she felt that she trembled, too.

"There's a lady who looks hurt." She pointed to an elderly woman, propped against a tree trunk, one claw-like hand holding her dressing gown together at the throat. An ambulance attendant bent over her.

Neighbors ran among the guests, offering their houses as shelter, rounding up the children and their parents and the old people first, throwing blankets around the shoulders of those who wore no coats.

Someone seized Clifton's arm and called his name and he turned to look into the anxious faces of Mary and her father. "Thank heaven you're all right!" Mary cried. "We got here as quickly as we could." She took Vicky's hand, forgetting the coat she carried. "You poor lamb! Your eyes are bright red."

"It's the smoke, that's all."

"Man, I'm glad to see you two." Clifton heard himself shouting. "How did you know it was the inn on fire?"

"I'll tell you," Tucker said shortly. "Come on, let's get you out of here." He herded them to the road, past the police cars sealing off the area in front of the entrance, down to the jam of parked cars. He found his own, almost hemmed in now.

Clifton and Vicky got in the back seat and Mary laid the coats beside them. "We thought you might have to get out so quickly you wouldn't have time to put anything on."

"We were lucky the fire started at the other end," Clifton told her while Tucker maneuvered the car out of its tight parking place, making a U-turn to head for home. "It gave us a little time to think."

"I just hope everyone got out," Vicky said hoarsely. The smoke still seemed heavy in her nostrils and her throat.

"You certainly had presence of mind to bring those," Mary said, pointing to the tennis rackets.

"I wish I'd thought of bringing my shorts. I was too scared, I guess," Vicky admitted. "I just saw the rackets and grabbed them."

"I'm sure you can wear my clothes," Mary told her. "We're almost the same size. If you don't mind tennis dresses."

"I'll try to get our things in the morning," Clifton said and, suddenly wearier than he had ever been, rested his head against the back of the seat until Tucker pulled the car up before the house.

Mrs. Tucker was waiting in a dressing gown at the front door. She took Vicky's hand and drew her into the hall. "I'm going to get you straight to bed. And Arthur, give Frank a stiff drink."

"Of course—"

"I have hot milk for you, Vicky—to help you sleep." She led her upstairs to a guest room where the bed was turned down and a nightgown and terry cloth bathrobe lay across the foot. Mary followed them into the room, but Vicky could see that Mrs. Tucker was taking charge as Aunt Nan would have done. "Get out of those smoky things," she ordered, and when Vicky had stripped, she handed them to Mary. "Put the coats in the kitchen, dear. They'll have to go to the cleaners."

"We're an awful lot of trouble," Vicky said in a small, apologetic voice, slipping the nightgown over her head.

"Not another word about that. Now get into bed and drink your milk."

Mary started to leave the room. At the doorway she paused. "I wish we could postpone your match. It doesn't seem right for you to have to play after a night like this," she said, regretfully.

"I wouldn't want you to," Vicky answered quickly.

"Whoever wins would have to play two matches on Saturday."

"That's true," Mary said. "We have to finish the tournament by then." She left then, and Mrs. Tucker perched on the edge of the bed to wait for Vicky to finish her milk.

"You're not to open your eyes until eleven. That will give you eight hours' sleep." She pushed a lock of hair back from Vicky's brow. "You'll have a good brunch and be fit as a fiddle for your match."

Vicky put the glass on the table and when Mrs. Tucker bent to kiss her cheek, she put her arms impulsively around her. "I love you, Mrs. Tucker," she whispered, and realized that she had never said that before to anyone, nor known the warmth and security of saying it.

"I love you, too, Vicky. You're a dear, courageous girl. You go right to sleep and don't worry about a thing. I'm just next door, if you need me." She turned out the light and went quietly from the room.

Once during the night, Vicky woke herself up with a cry. She put her hand over her mouth and hoped Mrs. Tucker hadn't heard her. Stiffly she lay listening and remembering part of her nightmare: crying children and the awful crush on the staircase, the flames shooting out from the dining room. Then she tried to relax. She took a deep breath and made her body sink into the mattress. When she closed her eyes again, she concentrated on an image of tennis balls flying back and forth across the net.

Vicky and Clifton, in borrowed clothes, were eating an eleven-thirty brunch of omelet and grilled tomatoes in the breakfast room when Mrs. Tucker came in and sat down with them. "How do you feel?" she asked.

"I haven't slept so long in years. I should have been up hours ago," Clifton said guiltily.

"You needed it. And you, Vicky?"

"Oh, I'm fine," Vicky lied, for she still felt tired, and her eyes felt bleary. She wouldn't admit it to anyone—not even to her father. It would only worry him, and he couldn't do anything about it. Perhaps by afternoon she'd feel better.

"I don't know whether or not Mary told you," Mrs. Tucker was saying, "but Arthur and I have to go to Long Island today."

"She mentioned it a few days ago," Clifton remembered.

"We feel dreadful about leaving you—especially not getting to see Vicky play. But we made our plans to leave a long time ago. It's our annual visit to Arthur's mother in Wainscott. She's quite old and hasn't been well and—you know how they are—they don't understand if you change plans."

"Please!" Clifton made a little interrupting gesture. "You couldn't have done more for us—letting us stay here. We're eternally grateful, really."

"Nonsense." She got down to business. "Arthur and Mary have gone to get your clothes and your car. He was on the phone early this morning to two or three people— there was something about insurance. Anyway, the rooms on your side of the inn didn't burn. And you'll be glad to know everyone got out."

"Thank God for that," he said with deep relief, and Vicky, too, felt that a prayer had been answered.

"I told Mary to take your things, and the coats you had on last night, to the one-day cleaner," Mrs. Tucker went on. "I'm sure everything must have smelled of smoke."

"My hair does, too," Vicky said. "I have to wash it."

"There's a shower in your bathroom," Mrs. Tucker told her, and continued, "Mary will let the cook know if there's something special Vicky eats before she plays—that is, tomorrow. I do hope the brunch is all right. I didn't think you'd feel like eating meat the first thing in the morning."

"It's fine. Just fine," Clifton said. "And thank you for your confidence in Vicky."

"She's going to win the tournament," Mrs. Tucker declared. "Mary said so."

If she gets through today, Clifton thought. If she just gets through today. "She's got the game to do it," he agreed.

At the sound of the opening door, Mrs. Tucker got up and went to the hall. Vicky and Clifton rose and followed her.

"We got everything," Tucker said with a proud grin. "And your car's outside," he added as Mary came through the doorway.

"That's just great!" Clifton cried.

"Here are the rest of your rackets, Vicky." Mary handed them to her. "They look all right, don't they?"

"Oh, yes." Vicky took them gratefully. "Thank you."

"I can get your clothes tomorrow at noon. The cleaning man thought he could get all the smoke out."

Tucker thrust a suit box at Clifton. "I think you'll find these fit a little better than my things." He looked down at the two or three inches of Clifton's exposed leg, and both men laughed. "You look like a country bumpkin in those pants."

"That's very nice of you, Arthur." He opened the box and took out tan gabardine slacks and jacket. "Hey, these are swell."

"Try them on," Tucker said.

"I'll be with you in a minute." Clifton took the clothes upstairs.

"You get back there and finish your brunch." Mrs. Tucker gave Vicky a gentle push, and Mary went with her to the breakfast room.

"I didn't get anything for you, Vicky. I knew my clothes would look well on you," Mary explained. "I'll have to give you that skirt and sweater. Hunter's green is marvelous with your eyes."

"Thank you for everything." Vicky thought that Aunt Nan couldn't have brought more order out of the terrible night than these kind people had done. She felt a silly lump in her throat as she tried to swallow the rest of her omelet.

When she had finished her brunch, Mary suggested, "Come on upstairs and try on my tennis clothes. We'll see which dress looks best." They met Clifton coming down the stairs.

"How do I look?" He turned around for their inspection.

"Very handsome," Mary said, and Clifton's heart gave a little leap. "Father hit your size right on the nose."

"You look nice, Dad," Vicky agreed. "Go show Mr. Tucker."

Clifton went on happily to the living room. Handsome, was he?

When Vicky and her father arrived at the club, followed by Mary in her own car, Gwen Stuart was waiting for them on the porch. She gave a little cry. "There you are! Oh, I'm so glad you're all right. I can't tell you how I worried when I heard about the fire on the radio this morning. I feel awful about not being able to postpone your match, Vicky. That was a dreadful thing for you to go through."

"She understands. She's a good sport about it," Mary told her.

"Of course, but—oh, dear. You must be exhausted." Gwen looked closely at Vicky as if to see fatigue in her face.

"I'm all right, really," Vicky said. She was very tired, but she didn't intend to admit it. She glanced at the grandstand court where Nancy Gilmore and Lucy Hammond were a set each.

Gwen went to her referee's table, picked up the morning paper and handed it to Vicky. "Did you see this?"

"No," Vicky shook her head. "I guess none of us thought about looking at the paper."

"It mentions you and your father at the end." Above the story, on the first page, was a picture of the inn burning. Vicky stared at it for a minute and then read the article as Mary and Clifton looked over her shoulder. When they had all read the final paragraph, "Vicky Clifton, the California junior champion and her father, Frank Clifton, former All-American football star, were among the inn's guests . . ." Clifton frowned. "I hope none of the wire services pick this up. It'll worry my sister sick."

Vicky looked up at him sharply. "Oh, Dad, you don't think they will, do you?" Of course Aunt Nan would be scared stiff, she thought.

"I don't know. They might think it would be of interest in San Francisco."

"Why don't you call her?" Mary suggested.

"I will when we get back to the house," Clifton said.

"And I can talk to her, too." Vicky hoped that she would be able to give her the good news that she had won. If she could just get through today.

"You'd better get dressed now," Clifton said, and she went to the locker room.

Players were dressing for a doubles semi-final. Two of them, partners whom Vicky didn't know, came over to her corner. "That was terrible about the fire. I'm sure glad you're all right," one of them said.

"I guess you're pretty tired," the other said, "but," she looked around her, "I hope you win."

"Me, too," her partner added.

"Gee, thanks," Vicky said, a smile breaking on her face, almost unable to believe what she had heard. She had felt the edge of friendship in their sympathy and wish for her to win. It was a strange and pleasant experience, and she wondered if she couldn't play just as well if she were friends with her opponents. And then she imagined her father's answer, "I want them to be afraid of you."

Ellen Basker came in to dress. "I heard about the fire. I'm glad you're okay."

"Thanks," Vicky said quietly. She finished dressing and left the room. The first semi-final had just ended and the players were coming off the court. Nancy Gilmore, the winner, looked tired but happy; Lucy Hammond, even tireder, managed a smile.

"Hey, Vicky!" She turned to see Julian coming toward her out of the crowd. "That was grim—last night—are you all right?"

"Sure," she answered, trying not to stare at him. "I'm fine."

"I went over there this morning. It was a shambles, except one side. Was that where your room was?"

"Yes. We were lucky."

"Did you get all your things out?" He was looking at Mary's dress. The knife-pleated skirt was a little too long for her, and the bodice was not quite tight enough.

"Mr. Tucker got them this morning, but they're at the cleaner's. This is Mary's dress."

"It's nice. You look great."

Pleasure welled up in her, and then she thought, You knucklehead, he's being polite.

Ellen came across the porch to them, slipped her arm proprietarily through her brother's. "Are you ready?" she asked Vicky.

"Yes." Vicky bit off the word. Now Julian was going out there to pull against her.

Gwen Stuart approached them. "Are you girls ready?"

"Yes," both said, and she led them to the court, Vicky behind her, Ellen and Julian following. At the courtside, having completed the little formality, Gwen left them. Vicky chose a racket from the three she carried, and put the others beside the umpire's stand. Then she turned to Ellen. Julian was talking to her quickly, at the edge of the court, with lowered head and serious eyes. Ellen nodded, he gave her shoulder a pat and moved off, looking for a seat. Vicky watched this brief scene jealously and then thought impatiently to herself, Of course he wants her to win. She's his sister, you goon.

The way Ellen began the match, Vicky thought she must be following Julian's instructions. Vicky imagined what they were: "She's got to be tired. Run her legs off. Don't give her a chance to get started." For Ellen, serving first, was wasting no time getting to the net, angling her volleys wide and deep, covering attempted passing shots easily with long stride and long reach, going back confidently to smash lobs, but coming in again to net.

When she had won the first game and they were changing sides, Vicky sensed the tension in the gallery, silent after its burst of applause. They're holding their breath for a breakthrough, she thought.

She served, and running up, found herself passed cleanly

down the sideline. Ellen's eye was "in" today. There was no doubt about that. And she liked pace. Vicky served wider, but that brought sharp, dipping returns and when she volleyed up, Ellen was waiting to put the ball away.

It was difficult to hear the score, 2–0, over the roar of the gallery when Ellen had won the game after six points.

Walking back to the baseline to receive service, Vicky told herself, "You know the answer to this—slow up the game." It would be more tiring in the long run to lengthen the rallies, wear down her opponent's patience. But she could play on the reserve energy that long training had stored up in her. One night like the last couldn't deplete it.

She began to lob her returns of serve so high and deep that Ellen, running up, was forced to turn and race back, and once there, she was pinned down with tantalizingly steady angled and line drives of depth but decreased pace. Trying to pound the paceless ball, she overhit; or, exasperated, took the ball too soon and found the net.

Reducing the pace on her serve, slicing it wide to forehand and backhand, Vicky discovered that Ellen couldn't hit the backward spinning ball down the line, and covering the crosscourt return she had a clear, straight volley into open court.

As Ellen's two-game lead disappeared, so did her confidence and her calmness. She played like someone in a pit, trying to scale the walls, finding the earth giving beneath her feet. With desperation came carelessness, mistimed shots, insecure overheads, and when Vicky began to attack her service fiercely again, she was too uncertain to come in for the volley. Vicky took over the net and, almost mercifully, ended the match without the loss of another game.

Afterwards, Julian looked as miserable as his sister. He pushed his way through the crowd to meet her as she came off court.

"I'm sorry, El. If she hadn't soft-balled you . . ." Vicky overheard him commiserate.

They were joined by Nancy Gilmore. "You would have beaten her if she'd *hit* the ball."

Ellen wiped her flushed, perspiring face with her towel, and the three walked on, unmindful of Vicky, who followed them. "I hope you beat her tomorrow." It was a plea, Vicky thought.

"So do I," Julian added with equal fervor.

Vicky dropped back. She didn't know why she had expected Julian to pull for her, once his sister was out of the tournament. She heard a "well-played" and several "congratulations" from the crowd as she passed through. But they seemed mechanical, as had the applause, at the end.

She looked for her father and saw him standing with Mary and Gwen Stuart on the porch. He looked as pleased as if she had already won the tournament. With a last, unhappy glance at Julian's blond head above the dispersing spectators, Vicky went across the lawn to them.

Mary greeted her with a rib-bruising hug. "You were wonderful, Vicky. I was silly enough to worry about you, after last night." She released her and looked at her with pride.

"*Nothing* bothers her," Gwen said admiringly.

"I'll never worry about you again," Clifton told her.

Vicky smiled at them, feeling a bit of pride herself and enjoying her victory at last. "You didn't show that you were worrying, Dad." She put her arm around her father's waist.

"You don't know how hard I tried not to," he grinned, and gave her damp, upturned cheek a kiss. "Go take your shower now."

"That's Dad's theme song," she said, and went off.

When Clifton telephoned Aunt Nan that evening at six o'clock, it was three o'clock California time and she had just come home from lunch with friends. From her surprise and delight at the sound of his voice, he knew that she had not heard about the fire, and that she had probably not heard of Vicky's win either. He decided to give her the good news first. "Vicky's in the final, Nan."

"Frank, how wonderful!" Her cry came over the phone like a squeal. Then her voice dropped to its normal level and she said calmly, "It doesn't surprise me a bit. I expect her to win the tournament."

"She only lost two games in her semi-final today, and—"

"Let me talk to her," Aunt Nan demanded. "I want to hear it from her."

"In just a minute. There's something else. There was a fire at the inn." He heard her gasp and went on quickly, "We're all right—the part we were in didn't burn. But we had to get out."

"When did this happen?" Her voice was so faint now he thought the connection was getting weak.

"Last night—or rather early this morning. Luckily friends of ours, the Tuckers, brought us to their house. We'll be here until the tournament's over."

He heard her breath escape in a long sigh. "And Vicky had to play after that?"

"You should have seen her, Nan. I've never been prouder."

"I want to talk to her."

Clifton turned over the phone to Vicky. "Hi, Aunt Nan. How are you?" Her voice rose as if it had to carry the breadth of the country without benefit of the instrument she held.

"How am *I*? How are *you*? Darling, are you really all right?"

"I'm fine. The Tuckers have been so nice to us, Aunt Nan."

"I'm sure they have. But aren't you exhausted?" Vicky detected the familiar concern, the "worrywart" voice.

"Not now. I feel full of pep," she told her truthfully. "I miss you," she added lovingly. "Here's Dad again." She handed the phone to her father and went from the library into the living room, where Mary waited.

"Was she terribly upset?" Mary asked.

"I guess so. Mostly about whether I was tired."

"Of course." Mary nodded. "She must be very proud of you for winning in spite of it. I am."

The next day Vicky saw the clipping lying on the bench in the corner when she went to the locker room to dress for her final match. But remembering her promise not to read anything about the tournament until it was over, she folded it and put it in her purse. Still, she was curious to know who had put it there. There was no one in the room. She had seen Nancy, dressed for the match, talking to friends on the porch. She wouldn't have done it. She hadn't even spoken to her during the tournament. Vicky shrugged. "So what?" she said aloud.

Nancy was obviously nervous. Vicky could sense it during the warm-up, and when the match began, she gave her no chance to get herself in hand. Finding a vulnerable low backhand, Vicky pounded the weakness mercilessly, and the sun-baked turf added such pace to her shots that she rarely had a return to volley when she went to the net. Even Nancy's service, usually powerful and reliable, was letting her down. Costly double-faults made her cautious, and when she softened her serve, Vicky was on it like a tigress.

At 30–40, match point, Vicky felt a tremor of excitement like an electric shock. In position to receive service, she looked down at her shoe tops for an instant, took a deep breath, then raised her head slowly. Nancy served deep to her forehand. Vicky thought it was out, started to let it go, then lunged at the ball. The return landed softly in mid-court. Nancy pounded it to the backhand corner and Vicky raced across the court. When she reached the ball, beyond the sideline, Nancy was crowding the net, waiting. Vicky's racket flashed in the sunlight, the ball sped from it, outside, but above the net post and clipped the corner of the court.

Applause rolled like thunder from the gallery. Whatever its sentiments had been, this was the winning shot of a real champion. Nancy, who had watched in disbelief as the ball flew by her, stood rooted to the court until Vicky ran to the net to shake hands.

"That was lucky," Vicky said, knowing it hadn't been entirely luck. She had aimed it there. She had to take the risk, for Nancy could have covered any other shot. The luck had been that the ball hadn't caromed off the post out of court.

"One point wouldn't have mattered. You were much too good." Nancy tried not to look as dejected as she felt, but her smile was thin. No one had ever beaten her 6–0, 6–0 before this.

As they posed for pictures during the presentation ceremony Vicky realized two things: by losing just five games in the tournament, she had probably set a record; and she was too good to play in the juniors again. What she didn't know, until later, was that she was the youngest player ever to win the title.

Julian was waiting at the edge of the crowd as she and Nancy left the court with their trophies. She saw the glance that passed between him and her defeated opponent —the disappointment in his eyes, the embarrassment in hers.

"I'm sorry, Nancy," he said softly, and fell in beside them. "You were too good, Vicky," he added. "No one could have beaten you."

"I was playing my best," she replied, and with a final, defiant look at his golden head and the cool smile in his gray eyes, she turned abruptly and hurried to her father and Mary, standing with Dan Neely, the *Eagle* reporter. She could see that her father was about to burst with pride, but he didn't gloat over her victory and she was glad of that. So many eyes were on them. Only Mary was unable to restrain her delight. She threw her arms around her. "I'm so thrilled!" she cried. "You were absolutely super."

"You set a couple of records today," Dan Neely said. Vicky feigned surprise, wanting him to tell her out loud. "You lost fewer games in the tournament than any winner ever has, and you're the youngest player to win the title. How's that for a first appearance in the national juniors?"

"I'm—glad." She had started to say proud.

"Will you defend your title next year?" he asked. "You'd probably win it a record number of times if you wanted to."

"I don't think so," Clifton answered for her. "I plan for her to step out of the juniors now."

This didn't seem to surprise Neely. "Makes sense," he remarked. "I hope I'm on hand when you win the women's."

It pleased her that he was impressed. He would write something nice about her.

16 It wasn't until Vicky and her father had gone back to the house, leaving Mary to her final duties at the club, that she remembered the clipping in her purse. "Someone put this on the bench where I dress," she explained, handing it to him. "I didn't read it, because I promised."

Clifton unfolded it and saw Maude Bagley's by-line. He sat down beside the French door in the living room to read it. Sitting opposite him, Vicky saw the muscles in his jaw tighten. "What does it say?" she asked apprehensively. He read on to himself without answering.

"To no one's great surprise, Vicky Clifton has reached the final round of the national junior tennis championship at the Philadelphia Cricket Club. It is the manner of her getting there that is astonishing in a thirteen-year-old, even one of Vicky's prodigious technical skill. She has lost just five games on the way and has left no doubt in anyone's mind that she is an athletic phenomenon with physical strength and emotional control beyond her years.

"Unfortunately, her popularity doesn't match these assets. But perhaps her father's stern disciplinary hand is at fault here. A well-known football star of the early fifties, he has instilled in her a will-to-win that has become a "killer instinct" and has kept her aloof from the other players.

Neither here nor in her native California does she appear to have a friend among her fellow competitors, nor does she seek friendships. She curtly refused the request of one of our leading juniors to practice with her before the tournament. She keeps to herself in a corner of the locker room, putting a barrier of silence between herself and the others. Her path as a champion will be a lonely one unless she comes to realize that there is more to sport than winning.

"If this seems like a strong indictment of her personality, it is written with equally great admiration of her incredible game . . ."

When Clifton had finished reading and started to put the clipping in his pocket, Vicky held out her hand. "I want to read it."

"There's no point in it," he answered roughly.

"I know it's awful. I can tell by your face. I want to read it anyway."

He handed it to her, got up and walked away. He couldn't bear to watch her face as she read it. "Remember, this is aimed at me," he said suddenly, in a imploring voice.

Her eyes went quickly from line to line of the blurring print. She felt her fingers clammy on the paper. When she had finished it, she handed it back to him, avoiding his glance. "They don't all hate me," she cried in a choking voice. "Two of them wanted me to win. They said so!" She fled upstairs to her room.

Left alone, Clifton's first impulse was to telephone Maude Bagley and tell her what he thought of her and her article. But common sense hammered at him. What good would that do? It's been done and read. It can't be undone. He wished he could think it wouldn't be remembered.

When Mary came home with a pile of telegrams that had arrived for Vicky at the club, she found Clifton, granite-faced, staring out the French doors in the living room. She put the telegrams on a table and went to him. "What's the matter? You look as if you could kill someone."

"I could." He took the article from his pocket. "Read this."

She read it slowly, frowning. Then she looked at him without expression. "Shall we throw it away?"

"I don't give a damn," he muttered.

"Frank, this is mild for her. I told you she could be vicious." She crumpled the clipping and threw it in the wastepaper basket.

"Mild!" he exploded. "To attack a thirteen-year-old like that without really knowing her at all?"

"You can't think of Vicky as a thirteen-year-old. She's a champion. For that reason alone she's vulnerable."

"Vulnerable? How?" His brows shot up like arcs over his angry eyes.

"Vulnerable to personal interpretations of everything she does. She's in the public domain now. There are the builders-up and the tearers-down. Maude Bagley is a tear-er-down. She always has been, by innuendo or otherwise. No one takes her seriously."

"Whoever put that article on the bench for Vicky to see took it seriously. Suppose she had read it before her match?"

"But she didn't, did she?"

"No, thank God. She kept her promise."

"Do you honestly think she would have lost, if she'd read it?"

He looked at her thoughtfully, his anger dimmed. "I don't know. She's a different kid on the court. She's got terrific concentration. But—I really don't know. It upset her enough when she read it to send her flying upstairs to her room. It's unfair. That's what bugs me. She keeps to herself in the locker room because she wants to be quiet before her matches. Is that so hard to understand? And *I'm* the one who doesn't want her making pals of the players, getting involved with them. *I'm* the one who won't let her practice with girls. I have my reasons."

"I'm sure you do. She's not run of the mill and she can't behave as if she is."

He ran his fingers roughly through his hair. "She's young. She's intense. I've got to keep her mind on a single track. We've got a tough goal. She can only make it one way."

"Frank—"

"Who does Bagley think she is, pussyfooting around cross-examining the players—and how does she know whether Vicky has friends in California or not?" Color mounted his cheeks.

"Please, Frank, take it easy," Mary pleaded. "Most people understand, but if you make so much of this, of course Vicky's going to think it's important. She should forget it. You both should."

"It's hopeless to tell a kid that."

"You can try," Mary said quietly. "Shall we take the telegrams up to her? They might cheer her up."

Clifton shrugged. "I guess so. I wanted to take you both to dinner—remember?"

"I've looked forward to it. Come on." She led the way to Vicky's room. But when Clifton said, "We're all going out for a bang-up dinner where there's music," Vicky shook her head.

"I don't want to go anywhere. I can do what I want tonight, can't I?" She looked from one to the other.

"Of course you can," Mary said. "Here's a st..ck of telegrams for you." She put them on the dressing table. "We can have a nice dinner here."

"No," Vicky protested. "I want you and Dad to go. I don't want you to stay home."

"We're not going to leave you alone," Clifton said flatly.

"That's what I want—please," Vicky begged and turned to the window.

Clifton looked helplessly at Mary. She motioned him from the room, then went to Vicky and put her arm lightly across her shoulders. "Part of being a champion is learning to roll with the punches," she said quietly. "There'll always be little people to snipe at you."

Vicky was silent.

"The only thing anyone is going to remember about this week is that you won the title. All the Bagleys in the world can't take that away from you."

Vicky gave her a slow, sidelong glance. "Aunt Nan won't see it, will she? Dad said the papers in San Francisco might write about the fire because we were in it. Do you think—"

"I threw it away. So unless you get another one and send it to your Aunt Nan, she isn't going to see it."

"Well, I'm not about to do that!"

"I wouldn't think so. There's a saying, Vicky. It's something like 'Today's newspaper is tomorrow's trash.' You don't have to remember any more of it than you want to. You're junior champion of the United States now and far more important than Maude Bagley or anything she writes. Will you forget about her?" She gave Vicky's shoulder a gentle squeeze.

"Yes, I'll try," she answered, brightening a little.

"And won't you come out and celebrate with us? It would please your father so much," Mary urged.

"I'd like to now. I'm sorry I flipped like that." Avoiding

Mary's eyes, Vicky went to the dressing table and picked up her telegrams.

"Read those and then get dressed. I'm starving."

"I'm not very hungry," Vicky said.

"You can have birdseed." Mary gave her a peck on the cheek and left the room.

Clifton was in the hall, leaning on the railing, gazing into the stairwell. "Vicky's going with us," Mary told him.

He stood up and grinned slowly at her. "Mary, I love you." It surprised him to see the faintest color come through the tan along her cheekbones. He wanted to say it again and again with its true meaning. But he couldn't— not yet. The next time he said it, it was to be a commitment. Before then, there were problems to be solved. Other lives than theirs were involved—Vicky's, Aunt Nan's.

As soon as they got home that night, Vicky said, "I had fun, Dad, but I'm tired. I'm going to bed now." She knew he'd like a little time alone with Mary. She had never seen him look as happy as he had when he was dancing with her, and she thought Mary looked as if she were on cloud nine. But she didn't want to think beyond that right now. To-morrow she and her father were leaving for New York City to see the sights, and for the beginning of the U.S. Open. That should keep his mind off Chestnut Hill.

The next morning Clifton stood beside the car door, his eyes fixed on Mary's face as if he wanted to imprint every feature of it indelibly on his mind. The sun, high in the east, flooded them with a hot, humid reminder that it was much later than he had planned to leave.

Vicky was sorry to leave, too, in a way, but New York and Forest Hills were waiting and she could hardly contain her excitement. Her father had said that they would leave at nine, and then he had sat forever over breakfast with Mary, and now she'd been standing on one foot and then the other for fifteen minutes while he said goodbye.

"Then you'll really come to the Open next year?" he asked, finally opening the car door.

"Yes—really," Mary said.

"That'll be cool," Vicky put in. She would like having Mary at the first national Open that she might play in. Her father seemed to take it for granted that the association would let her. Well, why not? After all, the *Enquirer* had written: "Incredible as it seems, she is ready to take on the women, and it is difficult to think of any in the first ten who wouldn't have a battle on their hands. It is certain that neither their names nor their games would intimidate this imperturbable thirteen-year-old."

Mary kissed her goodbye, and Vicky got into the car. "Come on, Dad," she called impatiently.

Clifton kissed Mary on the mouth and slid into the driver's seat.

17 The three days in New York and Forest Hills passed swiftly, but Vicky and her father had done so much that she was glad for the rest on the plane going home. New York City and the shops had been exciting, and the West Side Tennis Club at Forest Hills was as impressive as she had expected it to be with its great, concrete stadium.

She knew her father had missed Mary—she had, too— but it didn't dampen his enthusiasm for the matches. When the president of the club, Tom McCord, had taken them to his box in the stadium to watch the best players in the world, her father had asked as many questions about them as she had.

She had been particularly interested in the Australian champion, Nell Stanley, the favorite to win the tournament. Tall and strong, she hit like a man. But her height, Vicky had thought, should make it tiring for her to stoop to consistently low-bounding shots. This winter, she had decided, she would sharpen her sliced drives and drop shots, her short angled shots.

The top players, she had realized, were professionals, and when she and her father were back at the hotel that evening, she had announced, "I want to be a pro."

"The subject's premature," her father had snapped.

"Drop it, Vicky." And she had, but she didn't intend to let it rest there.

Although Vicky had told Mary that she would forget Maude Bagley and her article, she wished the reporter had seen her homecoming. Aunt Nan, to whose happy arms she rushed, was not the only one to greet her at the airport. There was Eddie, who kissed her boldly on the mouth; and Mr. and Mrs. Marsh; and Harlan Brooks, who presented her with a huge bouquet of American Beauty roses on behalf of the association; John Bartlett; Jerry, Bob, and Mike; Jack Kiley and Richard Cox with a photographer from the *News*, who took a picture of her alone, holding her roses and a racket, and another with Aunt Nan and her father and all her friends around her. Even a few strangers, meeting people at the airport, inquired whom all the fuss was about and joined the welcoming party long enough to congratulate her.

She had friends—wonderful, excited, and proud friends who knew and cared only that she had brought back the title she had been sent to win. Aunt Nan had a letter for her from the mayor telling her that San Francisco took pride in her accomplishment, and on the Saturday after her return, the San Francisco Tennis Club gave a luncheon in her honor at the Fairmont Hotel.

John Bartlett, who sat on one side of her, announced that she had been made an honorary life member of the club, and Jack Kiley, on behalf of the Banner Sporting Goods Company, presented her with a leather-bound clipping book containing all the articles about her for the year and bearing on the cover her name and the date in gilt letters. This pleased her more than anything else, and when she wondered at the thickness of it, Kiley explained that a clipping service had gathered the articles from all over the country. Aunt Nan, watching her, thought her face paled a little and was afraid the excitement was too much for her. Clifton, next to Aunt Nan, watched her, too, and knew the reason for her sudden pallor.

When the luncheon was over, Eddie asked if he could go home with her. "I'd like to look at your book," he said.

"You can come home with us, but I want to take a walk," she replied firmly. "It's nice outside. I don't want to sit in the house."

That seemed to satisfy him, and when they got in the car she clutched the book tightly at her side and got him to talk about himself—what he'd done while she was away.

"Gosh, it was only two weeks. I played tennis every day. And I thought about you a lot," he admitted with candor.

He's different, Vicky thought. He doesn't care who knows he loves me, but she didn't think that her father or Aunt Nan, keeping up a running conversation in the front seat, had heard.

As soon as they got to the apartment, Clifton took the book from her. "I want to have a look at this," he said, and gave her a meaningful glance. "If you and Eddie are going for a walk, you'd better change your shoes."

She didn't keep Eddie waiting long while she changed into blue jeans and sweater and loafers. She wanted to get him out of the house, away from the book.

Eddie seemed older and surer of himself with her, and this was ridiculous. It couldn't happen in two weeks. Maybe it was because he was in high school now, and that made him feel older and more important inside himself and she somehow felt it. As they walked toward Russian Hill where they would be able to see ships going through the

Golden Gate, he held her hand, swinging it lightly between them, without self-consciousness, as if it belonged in his.

"Did you make a lot of friends back East?" he asked.

"Some," she answered, and told him about the Tuckers. "After the fire—"

"That was awful," he interrupted, tightening his hand in a protective way around hers.

"Did you read about it? Aunt Nan said there was a little piece in the paper. We phoned her before it came out. We were afraid she'd be scared if she read it first."

"Sure I did. It was on the sports page." He slowed his step. "I would have died if you had gotten hurt." The words had the tone of a simple statement, as if he had said, "The sun's bright today." But they drew her eyes to his face, and although she knew he wouldn't die if anything happened to her, she could tell by his fleeting frown and the way he stared at the steep sidewalk that he would be terribly sad.

"Well, we didn't get hurt," she said.

"You must have been scared stiff."

She wanted to say, "I wasn't." Vicky Clifton didn't scare —that's what he and all the kids had learned and she liked it that way. But it wasn't true of that one time, and so she admitted, "I was, for a while."

Pushing on up the hill, they were silent for several minutes, except for their quickened breathing. Then he asked abruptly, "Did you meet any guys you liked?"

"One."

"Who is he?" His voice had a belligerent edge.

"Oh, someone from Princeton."

"College?" He laughed.

"What's so funny about that?"

"Well, he's old, isn't he?"

"What of it? I can like someone older than I am."

"Not that much older—you're only thirteen."

"I'm not always going to be thirteen. I'm going to be fourteen in two months. It wouldn't seem so much older if I was sixteen. Anyway, it doesn't matter. I don't like him now."

"Why not?" Eddie's voice lightened noticeably.

"He wanted me to lose."

"Come on!"

"Well, he wanted my opponent to win. That's the same thing."

"He sounds like a creep," Eddie said happily.

They came to the crest of the hill. He let go of her hand and they leaned against the retaining wall of a house to catch their breath. In the distance, the sunlight shone dully on the iron-oxide painted span of the bridge, but beneath it the water sparkled in shifting patterns, distorted by the wake of a fishing boat.

"This is the prettiest place in the whole country," she said with the sureness of a seasoned traveler. But Eddie wasn't listening. He had taken a gold signet ring from his left hand, and was turning it in his fingers.

"Will you wear this?" he asked, and held it out to her.

"It's new, isn't it?" She took it from him. The initials E.M. were engraved in it. "I've never seen it before."

"Dad gave it to me for my birthday."

"You can't give it away."

"I can give it to you."

She shook her head and handed it back.

"Won't you wear it?"

"No. It'd be silly."

"Why?" he demanded, hurt.

"Because it would look like we were going steady."

"I want to. Can't we?"

"I'm too young," she laughed, teasing. "You said I was only thirteen."

He ignored that and moved in front of her. "Don't you like me enough to?"

"Yes. But I'm not going to. Let's go back." It would have been easy to take his ring and say she'd go steady with him. Between school and tennis she didn't have time to do much more than they did together, anyway. But suppose she met someone she liked the way she had liked Julian—someone who gave her that queer feeling in the pit of her stomach and made her heart leap around like a jack rabbit. It would hurt him much more to find out, if he thought he had a claim on her. And there'd be the ring to remind her, every-time she looked at it.

Vicky started back down the hill and Eddie fell in beside her. He didn't hold her hand going back.

That evening Vicky had a chance to look casually at her clipping book, and she found a page where an article had been removed. Nothing remained but thin traces of paste. She closed the book. She'd never think about Miss Bagley's article again, and she'd never let anything unkind anyone wrote ever bother her.

"Would you like me to keep your book up to date for you?" Aunt Nan, who had taken up needlepoint, glanced up from the canvas. "There are two clippings to go in—the ones about your homecoming and the luncheon."

"And this squib," Clifton said, lowering the evening paper. Vicky looked over his shoulder at the small item he pointed to, and read aloud for Aunt Nan's benefit: "Vicky Clifton, the national junior champion, will not defend her title, according to a spokesman for the Northern California Tennis Association. She will confine her competition to women's events and will be entered in the U.S. Open next summer at Forest Hills."

"Hey, did you know about that, Dad?"

"I talked to Harlan Brooks about it at your luncheon. I was going to tell you—I didn't know it would be in the paper."

"And he didn't argue about it?"

"Not at all. The only argument we had was about the tournaments you'd play in before the Open. But I've made up my mind—two at the most. He'll come around."

"Your father and I agree you're going to concentrate on school now," Aunt Nan said firmly.

"I made that clear to Brooks. School and practice, period, until the term's over," Clifton stated.

"I'd like to give Tony some tennis lessons," Vicky threw in offhandedly.

Aunt Nan stuck her finger and gave a little cry.

"For the reason I think you do?" Clifton asked.

"It'd be good for him—" Vicky began, feeling her cheeks flush.

"As long as you do it for the right reason—not a feeling of guilt," her father said, "you can give him a lesson."

"I think it would be very nice," Aunt Nan said.

"Three lessons," Vicky said. "Serve, forehand, and backhand." She leveled her eyes at her father.

He nodded. "I told Brooks I'd have you ready to play the best women by summer. That means work-work-work on your game. That and school is all you can handle. So three lessons for Tony and no more."

"Okay," she promised.

At first, Vicky found it difficult to settle into the routine of school. The awe of her schoolmates embarrassed her. She missed Eddie, who could no longer meet her in the morning, and her mind kept wandering from her books to some high point in her tennis season. But as the novelty of having a champion in their midst wore off, her schoolmates paid less attention to her and stopped asking her questions about her matches, and she felt more natural. School, again, seemed a normal and acceptable part of her day.

True to her promise, she gave Tony just three tennis lessons, leaving the serve until last. By then she had discovered, by trying it herself, that if he tossed the ball up between his thumb and forefinger, he could keep it straight in the air. She wouldn't forget his delight when he hit the first serve into court, and connected solidly with his first drive. What he lacked in speed of foot, he made up for in determination, and almost reluctantly, she turned him over to Eddie, who agreed to rally with him once a week.

Eddie's game, as he had told her, had improved. But she was still able to beat him so easily that his confidence withered.

"Why can't I handle your short crosscourts?" he groaned, frustrated and angry at himself.

"You lunge at the ball because you don't anticipate it," she told him, but the explanation didn't correct the fault. When she caught him by surprise with the shot, following a deep line drive, he couldn't reach it any other way. It was a shot she had to sharpen, with Nell Stanley in mind, and she kept at it mercilessly. So when she told him that she couldn't play at Lafayette Square anymore, this time she thought he was relieved.

Vicky didn't know who told the *News* that she was giving Tony lessons, unless it was one of the players who stayed to watch after their game the first day, but on the third day a photographer appeared and asked her to pose tossing balls for Tony to hit. Tony clutched his racket like an axe and stood stiffly on the baseline. Vicky stood a few feet away from him.

"Pretend we're all by ourselves, Tony. Take it easy. It doesn't matter if you miss the ball. It won't show in the picture." She gave him a smile of encouragement, and when she saw his hand relax and the racket head drop, she nodded. Gently she tossed the ball, and to her surprise and his, he hit the best crosscourt drive he had ever made, even remembering to follow through. He hit several other shots less successfully, but it was the first forehand that appeared in the *News* the next day over the caption "Champion Teaches Young Tennis Hopeful." And that night Mrs. Mercati telephoned Vicky to thank her. Tony, she said with a soft laugh, had started a scrapbook.

18 On a Saturday afternoon in early May in a corner of the San Francisco Tennis Club lounge, Clifton paced the floor. "They've eviscerated the amateurs," he stated flatly. "Who's left of the top people to play in it? They're all pros."

"The national amateur will always be important," Harlan Brooks maintained heatedly. "It's a prestige title, and there'll be many very fine players in it." He shook his white head emphatically, and tried, by riveting his eyes on Clifton, to hold his attention.

Clifton looked out the window. He could see Vicky and Jerry playing. He was fascinated by the ease with which she was learning to increase the power and deception of her backhand smashes. He wished Brooks would leave him alone now. He had already made up his mind about Vicky's schedule.

"You can strike out half those tournaments." He turned his determined, rugged face to Brooks. "She will only play in the Eastern Grass Court, Merion, and the national Open—period."

Brooks made a visible effort to calm himself and alter his tactics. It was no good trying to dictate to this man. The florid color in his round cheeks subsided. He adopted a reasoning and persuasive tone of voice. "They want her at

Piping Rock, and you might say they *expect* her at the national amateurs. The experience would be tremendously valuable to her." He paused, then added pointedly, "Her first season in women's competition."

"What's the most important tournament in the country?" Clifton asked.

"The U.S. Open of course."

"That's what Vicky's pointing for. I told John Bartlett, when Vicky was just thirteen years old, that I'd make a champion of her in two years. This is the second year. I wasn't talking about the juniors. I meant top of the women, and that means the top title. She'll have to budget her energy."

"Aren't you pushing her pretty hard?" Brooks suggested.

"She'll be ready," Clifton said.

Brooks could see that Clifton's rigid opposition showed no signs of cracking, but he felt duty bound to deliver the balance of the association's proposed schedule. "We thought she might make her debut—shall we say—in women's tennis at the national hardcourt the end of May in Sacramento."

"She doesn't get out of school until June," Clifton reminded him. His expression grew more amiable. "Of course, she'll play in the Pacific Coast Open when she gets back."

"She'll be in school then," Brooks snapped.

"She'll be entering high school. But she can make up the work then. She won't be trying to prepare for a season."

"Well, I'm glad to hear she'll play in that," Brooks said with some acerbity.

Clifton stood up. "Vicky's practicing. Would you like to have a look at her?" he asked.

Brooks got slowly to his feet. "I guess that's all I will see her do until October." He gave a resigned sign. "I suppose you know what you're doing. She set a record in the juniors that'll be hard to beat."

When Jerry saw Clifton and Brooks coming toward the court, he caught the ball Vicky had just hit and called to her, "How about a set now?"

"You serve." She turned to take her position and saw her father and Brooks. Mr. Brooks looked very unhappy and she knew they had been talking about the tournaments and that her father had had his way.

Clifton had been pouring over the list of tournaments in the back of the tennis magazine for several nights, checking a half-dozen, consulting with Jerry on the phone about their relative importance. They had to fit the schedule he'd outlined, all hinging on the Open on August twenty-seventh, with a week to ten days rest and practice before the big one. Together they had come up with the Eastern Grasscourt at the Orange Lawn Tennis Club in New Jersey and the Pennsylvania Grasscourts at the Merion Cricket Club in successive weeks. They were both tough tournaments, Jerry had told him—just what she needed to prepare for the Open, and he agreed with Clifton that these two should be the limit.

When the decision was made and her father had explained it to her and to Aunt Nan, she had said, in a teasing voice, "Merion's not very far from Chestnut Hill, is it?"

"I don't know," he had snapped. "The club's in Haverford."

"Merion's where Julian was going to dinner the night we met him at the Tuckers'."

"Was it?" A slow flush had crept up his cheeks, and she had seen that Aunt Nan noticed it with a look of surprise.

When he had dropped the subject abruptly and had told her to go and do her homework, she knew she had embarrassed and angered him, and she had felt ashamed. He had a problem there, she supposed, on account of her and Aunt Nan.

Brooks was impressed with her practice. His face lit up with incredulous pleasure when she turned two "impossible gets" into winners and Jerry, startled, laughed and applauded her passing shots.

Clifton thought Vicky was showing off for Brooks, and the results pleased him. He had never seen her play so well from every part of the court, and when Brooks said afterwards, "She's matured as a player. She's fifteen better than when she came home," Clifton knew what he meant. She had an uncanny control of the ball, even though she had quickened her timing almost to the point of half-volleying, and she played with an even calmer confidence.

"I don't know a woman who could live against that tennis," Jerry stated proudly. "I went all out."

"How did you feel you were playing, Vicky?" her father asked.

"I'm not satisfied with my backhand smash down the line," she answered, frowning. "But I'll have it by July. I've got to get my right shoulder around more smoothly. There's a little jerk in it."

"It looked good to me," said Brooks, who had been a ranking player in his day.

"I want it to be perfect," Vicky told him.

"The way you work, I imagine it will be," Brooks said with willing admiration. They all had to realize, he thought, that this girl wasn't the usual junior preparing to challenge the women's field.

When Vicky and her father got home, Aunt Nan told her that Eddie had phoned and wanted her to go to the movies.

"How are they going to get there?" Clifton asked. "I'm not going to have her on the street at night with a kid."

"Oh, Dad—" Vicky protested.

"Don't 'Oh, Dad' me, with the things that go on in this place—"

"Calm down, Frank," Aunt Nan admonished. "Mr. Marsh is going to drive them and pick them up afterwards. I told Eddie she'd go if he didn't hear from her."

"You can't go on treating me like a baby," Vicky complained.

Clifton's eyes blazed. "I'll protect you as long as I can. Read the papers, any day of the week—the things that happen to kids *and* grownups even in broad daylight—"

"You're such a gloom bug, Dad."

"They're coming for you at eight-thirty," Aunt Nan said.

"Why can't they go to the early show?" Clifton grumbled. "Vicky's playing tomorrow."

Aunt Nan sighed deeply and shook her head at her brother. "For heaven's sake, what difference does it make, once in a while? She can sleep late in the morning. Perhaps the Marshes have dinner later than we do. Maybe it isn't convenient for Mr. Marsh to drive them earlier. I didn't ask!"

"All right, all right." Clifton raised his hand. "I give in."

Vicky went to her room to unpack her tennis bag.

Alone with her brother, Aunt Nan said, "Vicky's going to get sick of tennis if you don't let up on the reins now and then. Most fourteen-year-olds—"

"Please don't tell me what most fourteen-year-olds do. I'm well aware of it."

"I don't mean the undisciplined ones."

"Drop it, Nan. I know what you mean."

Later, after Eddie had called for Vicky, Clifton exploded, "Why couldn't she wear a dress? Why does she have to go out at night in those pants!"

"Because all the girls do. At least she doesn't have her shirttail hanging out. Let's talk about something pleasant, Frank. Tell me about Mary."

His face went red, then slowly the color drained out of it. He went to the window and stared, frowning, at the bay. "What about her?" he asked.

"Have you fallen in love with her?"

"Yes." He spoke as if to himself, almost in a whisper.

"What does she look like? Tell me about her."

"She's about your height, dark hair, dark eyes, lovely figure. She's kind, understanding." He swung around. "She's altogether beautiful." He saw compassion and affection in his sister's face.

"What are you going to do about it?" she asked.

"Nothing," he said. "Yet."

"Because of Vicky?"

"Partly—"

"Good Lord, Frank, you're not thinking of me, too, are you?"

"Why shouldn't I? You're part of our life. You've been like a mother to Vicky."

"Naturally. I love her. But that's beside the point. I think you ought to get married again. You're young. And Vicky seems to like Mary."

Clifton thrust his hands in his trouser pockets. His troubled eyes seemed to look through her. "I know she does. But liking her is one thing. Breaking up our family life is another. I don't want to do anything that's going to throw her off balance at this point."

"Have you talked to Mary about it?"

"No."

"If she's as attractive as you say, Frank—"

"I know. Some other guy will come along."

"Exactly. Has she ever been married?"

"She was engaged. He was killed."

"Would you like me to talk to Vicky?"

"No!" He jerked his hands from his pockets and sat down beside her on the sofa. "I don't want you to do that, Nan."

She took his hand and was surprised to find it cold. "Do you *want* to get married again?" she asked.

"Yes—to her. At the right time. If she'll have me."

"What do you think the right time is?"

"After Vicky's won the Open—when my job with her is finished. When we can plan so that everybody's happy."

Aunt Nan shook her head disapprovingly. "I've never heard of anything so stupid. It might be two or three years before Vicky is good enough to win the Open. It's unfair to her to put that kind of condition on your own happiness. After the tennis season—yes. But not the other. Not the unreasonable."

"You haven't seen her play." Clifton withdrew his hand and turned to face her. "She's fantastic."

"But she'll be playing experienced women champions. The physical strain alone will be much greater. It really worries me."

"She's strong, Nan, and she knows how to conserve her energy. Next Saturday, I'll take you to watch her play with the pro. You'll see I'm right."

"I hope you are," Aunt Nan said, unconvinced. "As right as I think I am about you and Mary. Will you give that some thought?"

He nodded. "After the Open."

"I want to be a pro. Do you think that's crazy?" Seated between Eddie and his father in the car on the way home, Vicky looked at one and then the other.

"I would, too," Eddie said. "They're making a lot of money."

"How would you fit pro tennis in with your schoolwork? They're on the go all the time, aren't they?" Marsh inquired cautiously.

"Oh, I wouldn't want to join one of those pro groups. I'd be an independent pro and play when I pleased," she said.

"I don't know much about it, but I don't suppose it's very different from being a young movie actress," Marsh conceded.

That struck Vicky as an argument to use with her father. She hadn't thought of it, herself, but it was true. There were lots of kids much younger than she who were actors and actresses and made a lot of money. Well, the court was her stage.

"I imagine you'd have to do pretty well in the women's tournaments before you'd qualify as a pro," Marsh suggested.

"I don't think you have to do anything but say you're a pro," Vicky told him, not really knowing, but remembering that she'd read something about it in the tennis magazine. "You can't suddenly decide to play for prize money in the middle of a tournament, though. And you've got to be good enough to get in the big tournaments in the first place."

"You don't have to worry about that," said Eddie, as his father pulled the big Lincoln up in front of Vicky's apartment. At the front door, in the recessed entrance, he took her hand. "I hope you turn pro. I think you'd be right to do it," he told her.

"You do—honest?" She looked up at him with eyes bright and questioning in the overhead light.

Solemnly, he nodded and then moving close to her, he bent his head and kissed her softly. His mouth lingered for a moment on hers, and when he raised his head, he was surprised to see a look of confusion in her gaze and a warm flush in her cheeks before she turned from him, quickly unlocked the door and ran across the hall to the elevator.

He stood there, lost in wonder, until a short beep of the car horn told him that his father was impatiently waiting.

Why tonight? he kept asking himself as they drove home. He'd never figure Vicky out. But he was too happy to care.

In the elevator, Vicky pushed the button for her floor and leaned against the wall as the car crawled slowly up. She tried to clear her mind. Why had this happened to her? Eddie was the same boy he had been on the hill, and yet he wasn't to her now. But she didn't know why. When he had kissed her, she had wanted to put her arms around his neck and make him keep his mouth on hers and even thinking of it now gave her a little spasm of pleasure. Eddie! It was wild.

She found her father and Aunt Nan waiting up for her, but she knew she couldn't make sense tonight about turning pro. The discussion would have to wait until tomorrow. Anyway, they both looked tired, her father particularly, as if something worried him.

"Was the picture good?" Aunt Nan asked her, noticing her high color but not commenting on it.

"I liked it. But it was long. You didn't have to wait up for me."

Her father got up and stretched his back. "If you're going to stay out till midnight—"

"Now, Frank—" Aunt Nan warned.

Vicky kissed them goodnight and went to bed.

The next night, after an afternoon of intensive practice that had wiped all thoughts of Eddie from her mind, she asked her father about turning pro. "I'd have to play in the Opens anyway, to get the best competition. What's the point in playing as an amateur?"

"In your case, I don't suppose there is much point," Clifton conceded. "But I don't want you to be premature about it."

"You're so young to be a pro, Vicky," Aunt Nan voiced her objection in a plaintive voice.

"There are lots of movie actresses who are younger than I am. They're pros at what they do," Vicky countered, playing her trump card.

That silenced Aunt Nan, but her father would go no further than compromise. "I'll make a deal with you," he said. "If you win at Orange, you can turn pro. Doesn't that sound fair, Nan?"

"I suppose I'll get used to it," she said.

"That's fair, Dad," Vicky agreed.

The weeks passed swiftly into July. Eddie was at the airport with Aunt Nan to say goodbye to Vicky. He looked bereft for he had seen little of her since the night they had gone to the movies, but he hadn't dared complain when she made the excuse that she was in training. He knew what the summer meant to her. When he started to kiss her goodbye, she gave him her cheek, and then she was gone. He and Aunt Nan watched the plane until it was a speck in the sky.

When Aunt Nan drove him home, she said, "Don't be sad, Eddie. She'll be home before you know it."

"It won't make any difference," he mumbled.

She gave his hand an affectionate pat. "She's under a lot of pressure. She's indifferent to everything but tennis now. Just be patient. You know she's fond of you."

"I guess that's what it is—really," he said, and lapsed into glum silence. He'd give a lot to know what Vicky had said to her aunt to make her feel sorry for him. It wasn't just what Miss Clifton said about being patient. It was the pat on his hand as if she were comforting a disappointed small boy.

19 After four days at Forest Hills for practice on grass, Vicky went through the early rounds at Orange with a dispatch that focused the attention of the press on her. Nell Stanley, the Australian champion, was not competing, and an injury to the ranking American pro, Jean Maguire, had forced her to withdraw. But Evelyn Drury, last year's surprise winner of the national Open, was entered, and it looked as if the English player might have the task of turning the junior champion back in the final.

Vicky allowed none of her opponents to play their games; and her opponents complained of her angles, her accuracy, and her depth. It was clear to the onlookers that if a player liked to hit flat shots, Vicky gave her heavy underspin; if she hit the low ball best, she gave her top-spin. And she made all of them cover court until fatigue slowed their legs and their pace, and many of her placements were unpursued.

It came as no surprise to anyone when she reached the final with Evelyn Drury. The grandstand was packed to capacity. A hush fell over the spectators as the match was about to begin.

Winning meant more than a title to Vicky. She had reminded her father of his promise to let her turn pro if she won the tournament, and he had neither wish nor reason to reargue the point, now.

Waiting for the umpire to call play, Vicky glanced at the colorful mass of spectators in the west stand. The applause, when she had made a spectacular shot or won a hard-fought game, had rolled down like thunder. And after her semi-final victory they had given her a standing ovation as she had left the court. Although she hadn't lost a set, so far, she wondered if they thought now that she had already done more than should have been expected of her and was about to be put in her place by the lithe, brilliantly aggressive, dark-haired player across the net.

The other players had treated her somewhat that way. They had been generous in their congratulations after the quarters. One of them had said to her, "You've played a great tournament," as if her winning streak were over. But after she had won her semi-final, she heard her opponent say to a commiserating friend, ". . . beaten by a fourteen-year-old junior! I'd better quit playing."

Now, looking across at Evelyn, Vicky supposed she felt that her reputation rested squarely on this match. It wouldn't surprise her if all her ex-opponents were pulling for Evelyn, even though players usually liked to see the person win who had beaten them.

Because Evelyn had lost in an early round at Wimbledon, Vicky suspected that, like many brilliant players of whom she'd read, she was either very good or very bad. The quality of her game would depend on her touch and her confidence. She wasn't a plugger. If she was forced to miss shots she usually made with ease or if she was kept from the net, where the main strength of her attack lay, her game might fall apart.

The umpire called play. Vicky served an ace down the

center line. Evelyn smiled and walked to the left court, as if she were thinking it was good to have aces expended early in the match.

Suddenly Vicky saw not Evelyn but Jerry Potter on the other side, and she said to herself, knowing what Jerry would advise, "Plan every shot to get to the net." And she did. Hitting for the corners, scant inches inside the lines, her volleys following service had a crisp finality. When Evelyn came to net behind her own service, Vicky caught her at her feet with the sharp, short crosscourts she had practiced so long and arduously; or tossed up pinpoint lobs that fell on the baseline, sent her opponent scurrying for them, and gave herself the net position. She expected every shot to come back, as she did when she played Jerry.

Vicky made errors. They were inevitable, playing the ball as close to the lines and the net as she was. But they contributed only two games to Evelyn, as Vicky ran out the set.

Evelyn was shaking her head, talking to herself, taking chances now in a desperate effort to elude Vicky's flashing racket, for in the interchange of shots Vicky inevitably worked out her pattern, made the opening for the winning placement.

Then, at 2–5 on Evelyn's serve, as if someone had called to her, "Slow the pace," she began to lob. Instead of going in behind her service, she stayed back, and when Vicky came in behind her service return, up went the ball. Evelyn had trouble getting the depth to make the shot an outright winner, or to force Vicky to take the ball on the bounce. Once Vicky overhit her smash, aiming for the backhand corner. A second smash, biting into the turf, was unreturnable. At 15–all she hit a half-dozen overheads to left, to right, but relentlessly a lob floated back until one, closer to the net, enabled her to angle it off the sideline into the stands for 15–30. A spectator caught it. The ballboy at the umpire's stand turned to the gallery, waiting for the ball to be thrown back to him. But when he heard Evelyn serve, he swung around to his post at the net. The serve hit the net tape and rolled back on the court. The ballboy retrieved it and scuttled back to position. The second serve, down the center line, was good. Vicky drove a backhand deep to Evelyn's left corner and went up. This point, one of the most important in any game, she was determined to win. 15–40 would give her two match points. Her nervous, disgusted opponent, on the verge of defeat, would tighten up.

Back came a lob, just beyond the service line. Vicky ran backward to cover it. As she leapt into the air, extended to hit it at arm's length, another ball came into her vision. The spectator, thoughtlessly, had tossed back the ball he had caught. Involuntarily, her eyes shifted from the lob for a split second, she hit late and off-balance and when she came down, felt her foot slipping from under her. She dropped her racket, put out her hand to break her fall and collapsed onto it. The ball, hitting the tape, fell into Evelyn's court. Searing pain shot up her arm. She lay still on the court for a moment, afraid to move. Then slowly she sat up. The service lineswoman rushed from her chair and knelt down beside her.

"Have you hurt yourself?" she cried.

It seemed to Vicky that she screamed at her. She shook her head to clear it and got up. "I've hurt my wrist," she answered, holding the throbbing joint. Her arm felt ablaze with pain from fingertips to elbow.

Evelyn had run to her now and hovered solicitously at her side. "What did you do?" A damp curl was plastered to her forehead above her anxious blue eyes. Vicky tried to smile, and at the same time, she felt moisture gathering in the corners of her eyes. Embarrassed by it, she looked down at her arm and raised her fingers from her wrist. It was beginning to swell. "Do you think you broke it?" Evelyn asked, staring at it aghast.

"I don't know. I've never broken a bone before," Vicky answered.

Clifton had come from the stands and was hurrying to her, and the umpire, climbing down from his chair, joined them. Clifton looked dolefully at her wrist. "I guess that puts you on the bench for a while, darling." He slipped his arm comfortingly around her waist and glanced at Evelyn. "I'm sorry, Miss Drury." Gallery voices drifted down to them in a hum. "Obviously, she can't go on," he told the umpire.

The umpire frowned. "Of course not. It's a rotten shame."

Vicky looked at Evelyn with despair and disappointment. "I'm sorry," she mumbled.

"You had me beaten." Evelyn picked the racket up from the court and handed it to Clifton.

Vicky shook her head. "It wasn't the last point."

"Come on, Vicky. I'm going to get you to a doctor." Clifton started to take her from the court, when the umpire broke in. "We have a doctor here—one of the club members. I'll get him." As Vicky and her father went toward the locker house, close by the courts, they heard his voice booming over the loudspeaker, requesting Doctor Simpson to go to the ladies' dressing room, and then intoning the score, 6–2, 5–2, default.

Shortly after Clifton left Vicky at the dressing room door, Evelyn appeared. "I've got Vicky's sweater and the rest of her rackets. I'll pack her things for her."

"I'll take the rackets," he said and gave her a grateful smile. "And Miss Drury—thank you."

Evelyn opened the door, paused with her hand on the knob. "You can be proud of her, Mr. Clifton. Everybody knows she would have won."

Waiting outside the room, Clifton was besieged by press, tournament committee women, and two of Vicky's former opponents, all concerned, but especially curious about the effect of the injury on her season.

"I don't know. The doctor's with her now," he repeated over and over, and when thin, dour Dr. Simpson came from the room, they stepped away to let Clifton speak privately with him. As soon as the doctor walked off, they crowded in again. Relief was clear in Clifton's face, taut and thin-lipped a few minutes before. "It's a sprain," he told his listeners. "She'll be out until the Open."

"It's definite then—she'll be able to play the Open?" a reporter asked.

"That's what the doctor thinks," Clifton told him. He didn't add that she'd have just four days to get back in shape before the tournament.

"Is there anything we can do?" one of the committee women asked.

"Not a thing, thank you," Clifton answered, looking impatiently over her head at the dressing room door.

Driving to the Greenwood, on the outskirts of South Orange, Clifton glanced at Vicky, silent beside him, her bandaged wrist resting in a sling. There was a pinched look about her face, a whiteness around her compressed lips.

"Does it hurt pretty bad, Vicky?" he asked.

She nodded. "The doctor gave me some pills for pain. I took one, but it doesn't seem to help much."

"You're going to be all right. I've had a lot of sprains in my day. I'll bet I've played as many football games with strapped limbs as without," he said with a labored smile. But much as he tried to reassure her, and she wished to be reassured, it was clear to him that anxiety was oppressive in her. "We'll have it X-rayed—just to be sure," he decided.

"Here?" she asked.

"Why not?"

"I want to get out of here." She didn't know why she had made it sound so urgent, as if she hadn't enjoyed herself until this happened, and she added quickly, "I don't mean I didn't like it here—"

"I know," he interrupted. "Do you feel like driving? Would you like to go to Forest Hills this afternoon and get settled in?"

"Oh, yes, I would."

"Then we'll go as soon as I get us packed."

She was silent again for some time, and then she said quietly, but firmly, "I want to be friends with the players. They were so nice to me."

Clifton said nothing.

"Don't you see, Dad? They don't treat me like I'm some kind of a freak. I don't have to hang around with them all the time to be friends with them."

"I didn't notice you hanging around with them at all. When did you make this decision?" he asked, warning himself not to upset her, not to get into an argument at a time like this.

"In the dressing room. We all talked. They were just— friendly. Even the ones I beat. And I didn't try to keep to myself—and I nearly won," she finished.

"I think it's more important than ever now for you to

keep yourself aloof, for them to fear you. You've given them good reason to."

"Well, they don't, and that doesn't keep me from beating them. And I like it that way."

Clifton disregarded his self-imposed warning. "Maybe you don't need me at all. Maybe Aunt Nan can take over. I'll get her back here—"

"You're mad at me." Vicky fixed her eyes on the road. "I didn't mean that, but it would be nice if Aunt Nan could come to the Open, wouldn't it?"

"Yes," he answered after a moment and knew that he had come to the end of the line. Vicky was her own girl now.

"I'd better call Mary," Clifton said, as he packed their clothes. "She was planning to come to Merion to see you play."

"How do you know, Dad?" From her armchair by the window, Vicky cast a suspicious eye at him.

"She wrote that she was, when I told her we were going there."

"Oh. Did you write to her a lot?"

"No, not a lot."

"Did she write a lot to you?"

"No. Two or three times."

"Why didn't you tell me?" Vicky's mouth drew down in a pout.

"They were written to me," he said.

She accepted the rebuke in silence.

There was an angry edge to his voice when he phoned Mary, and she knew Mary had noticed it when her father said, "I'm sorry—I *am* upset. Vicky's sprained her wrist. She won't be able to play for a couple of weeks." Then he was silent for several moments, listening, shaking his head.

"We can't. That's sweet of you, Mary, but we're going to Forest Hills. Vicky wants to get settled in, and I want to get her wrist X-rayed . . . Yes, I'm sure you have a good doctor there, but I want to get someone in Forest Hills who can keep an eye on her when she starts practicing. . . . I'll miss you, too. You promised to come to Forest Hills. Don't forget."

When he hung up the phone, he avoided Vicky's eyes and returned to packing.

She watched him until he had almost finished and then asked. "How about Aunt Nan? Aren't you going to call her, too—so she won't worry?"

Clifton turned to her, a dress half-folded in his hands. "Of course. As soon as the rates come on tonight." For an instant their eyes met and held. Then she closed hers and rested her head against the back of the chair.

20 Dr. Green's office was in his Tudor home, a replica of many others in Forest Hills. He X-rayed Vicky's wrist, found no break, and assured Clifton that she would be playing as well as ever in two weeks' time. "Hot Epsom salts soakings," he prescribed. "She can take the sling off in a week. And she can wear an Ace bandage instead of that tape."

"That's the same treatment I used to have," Clifton told her, walking back to the Forest Hills Inn. "I told you you'd be all right. We'll take long walks for exercise—"

"*Some* exercise," Vicky said.

"It's the best, for your legs. And we can drive out to the country and find us a hill."

"This place is sure flat. Crazy name for it."

They passed under the enclosed bridge-like structure that connected the tower wing and main building of the Inn. "You go up to our rooms. I'll get the Epsom salts," Clifton said.

She walked past the tables on the sidewalk cafe and into the lobby. It was almost empty of guests. Before long it would be teeming with tennis players with high hopes, and little by little they would dwindle away, most of the hopes shattered for this year. She felt a radiating pain in her wrist and wondered if the doctor knew what he was talking about—if she would really be as good as ever when she began to play again. The way her wrist felt now, she couldn't even imagine gripping a racket without a quiver in her stomach.

At six o'clock, Clifton phoned Aunt Nan, and to Vicky's surprise she found that her father had been serious about having her come East. "We both miss you. Vicky was talking about it today. She'd like you to come for the Open. . . . Of course I would, too, Nan. . . . That's nonsense. Here, talk to Vicky." He held out the phone and Vicky took it eagerly.

"Oh, Aunt Nan, would you come!" she cried.

"Not this time, darling. Next year," Aunt Nan said in her determined voice. "I'd be so excited you couldn't help but feel it and I don't want anything to distract you. Your father's done wonders with you. It's far better for you to be with him alone."

"But—" She started to say that Mary was coming up and, catching herself in time, finished, "it would be such fun to have you. Especially if I win."

"Next year. I promise. But not this time," Aunt Nan said firmly. "May I speak to Frank again?"

She wanted to know more about Vicky's injury, what was being done for it, if the doctor was the best he could get. Finally, impatiently, Clifton said, "Look, Nan, I called you so you *wouldn't* worry, not so you *would*. Vicky's going to be fine. I'm going to hang up now. I'll keep you posted by letter. No, of course I wouldn't let her play if her wrist wasn't well enough. It's only a sprain, dear, a simple sprain. Goodbye now." He put down the phone. "God! What a worrywart," he cried out. Then, shaking his head, he smiled. "Okay, let's go to dinner." Walking to the elevator, he put his arm across her shoulder. "I'm sorry Aunt Nan won't come," he said.

Vicky reached for his hand. "I guess she's right."

Vicky brought the subject up casually. She and her father were walking past the stadium on one of their long daily walks. It was a week before the Open, the sling was off her arm, and in three days she would begin to practice. "It's going to be exciting playing here," she said, looking up at one of the stone eagles perched on the rim of the arched concrete wall.

He followed her glance. "Are you going to make the eagles scream, Vicky?"

"I hope so. Dad, you said I would have won at Orange if I hadn't hurt myself."

"You would have had to fall apart not to, and you don't fall apart," he answered.

"Then just on account of my accident, I don't get to turn pro?"

She waited for him to take the bait. It was a few minutes before he replied, "I've been giving that some thought. Will you answer me a question honestly?"

"Of course. I always tell you the truth."

"I know. But I want you to *think* before you answer. Would playing for money put more pressure on you than playing just for the glory of it?"

"It wouldn't put any pressure on me at all. I swear it. When I'm on the court I never think of anything except what I'm doing."

"I believe that," he said. "All right. I'll phone Harlan Brooks—that's only courteous. And then I'll ask Mr. McCord to do whatever's necessary about it. He'll know who to tell."

So it was arranged, and the news item was in the *New York Times*. Other than that, there was little comment about it. Turning pro had lost the novelty it once had. It didn't surprise Vicky when she went to the club for her first day's practice and ran into Chris Stafford coming off court after a game to learn that she, too, had turned pro at the beginning of the season.

At Clifton's request, Dr. Green accompanied them to watch Vicky's practice and check on her wrist. He stopped her once during her game with the pro. "You're hitting the ball as if you're afraid of your wrist," he observed. "Does it hurt you?"

"No, it doesn't," she answered. "But I guess I expect it to."

"Then forget it," he said sternly. "Keep the Ace bandage on if it will give you more confidence in it. But *hit* the ball!"

She did, and that was the last time she worried about her wrist.

During her practice the day before the tournament started, Vicky noticed a group of men standing with her father and McCord on the terrace watching her. Officials, she thought, and was glad that she was playing well, making the pro scurry to win his points, hitting line drives that kicked up the chalk and whipping her short, angled returns like a lash, out of his reach.

When she had finished and joined her father, she found that she had been right, and the men, impressed with her, were lavish in their praise. "You'll go far in the Open if you keep that up," Gary Cross, the good-looking, dark-haired tournament director, predicted.

Vicky thanked him. She didn't know what he meant by "far," but she knew what it meant to her.

McCord introduced her to the others: Joseph Hancock, the president of the United States Lawn Tennis Association, a quiet, tall, blond man with a shy smile; and Kenneth Bruce, the tournament referee, short, ruddy-faced, with crisp sandy hair and a penetrating glance.

"I never saw anyone move with less effort than you do," Bruce said. "You have amazing anticipation."

Vicky gave him an appreciative smile.

"You know, I thought you were premature turning professional," Hancock told her, "but I'm not sure I was right, now."

Her father looked embarrassed. "She was determined to," he said.

Bruce nodded. "I can't say I blame her."

Her father told her later that these men were the big guns of the tournament. "I think they had a hard time believing their eyes when they saw you play, Vicky. Mr. Hancock began talking about Wimbledon next year. They all think you're ready for it."

"Wow!" Vicky cried softly.

Vicky had a strange and disturbing reaction to the tournament when it began. The crowds that had been part of the excitement of the Open for her the year before seemed oppressive now—not those in the stadium or the grandstand, but the milling crush of people in the alleys between the field courts, on the paths, in the clubhouse, at the refreshment stands. Everything from the corporate pavilions to the IBM Computer Scoreboard and the clacking typewriters in the marquee seemed to scream THIS IS BIG TENNIS. Bustling, badge-wearing officials, perspiring, serious-faced players, intoning umpires, hunched-over linesmen, scurrying ballboys gave the scene an atmosphere of intense importance.

Vicky felt as if there were no escape from it, no place except her room at the inn where she could be quiet and think before her match. The crowded dressing room was an extension of the outside activity. She had come here a half hour early to dress leisurely for her two-thirty match, and now she wished that she had dressed at the inn. She would from now on, and bring a change of clothes in case her match went to three sets. Thinking of that, she wondered how she'd feel during an intermission. Never having lost a set, it would be a strange experience. Would she let down? Would she stiffen up? Could she resummon her concentration?

"What kind of a draw have you got?" someone asked her.

She looked up at her questioner, a slight, olive-skinned player. One of the foreign players, she thought. "I haven't studied it," she answered.

The player gave her a dubious frown and went on dressing.

It was true. Her father had a copy of it, though. He had broken his rule because, he said, he wanted to make a record of the women's matches. He didn't say why, and she didn't ask to see the draw. It had become almost a superstition with her not to look at it until the last rounds. Her father simply told her whom she played and when. But in the dressing room it was impossible not to hear, unless you were deaf, who won, who lost, how they took it; to hear of the good breaks, the bad breaks, the blind linesmen. In the nearly half hour she had been here, she had heard some of all of this, but she had seen that several of the players, going about their dressing or undressing, were quiet and indifferent to it, as she wanted to be.

Being a part of the tournament that included the best men and women players in the world was quite different than being the potential entry that she had been last year when she came here to see what it was like. She wasn't seeking a place to think quietly then. She had been part of the spectator scene.

"Hello, Vicky. How's your wrist?" Evelyn Drury dropped down beside her on the bench.

"Hi!" Vicky was happy to see her and gave her a warm smile. Evelyn was largely responsible for her conclusion that having tennis friends was important to her.

"You've got an easy draw, haven't you? No one until you meet Mercier in the quarters."

"Who's she?" Vicky asked. She put on her shoes and pulled the laces tight.

"The French number one," Evelyn replied, surprised that she didn't know. "Haven't you studied the draw?"

"I never do," Vicky said casually. "I take them as they come."

"Not a bad idea. I don't suppose it really helps you to know who you're going to play three rounds from now— if you get there."

"That's what I think. It's like figuring on someone's weak backhand, and they hit it like a streak when you play them. You've got to figure where they're weak that particular day." She realized that she had never discussed anything like this with a fellow competitor before.

"It's like Orange," Evelyn said.

"What do you mean?" Vicky sat up, curious.

"Everyone told me you weren't experienced enough to stand up under a constant net attack—that the pressure would break your game." She laughed. "You just took the net away from me. It was as simple as that." She stood up. "I've got to get dressed. Good luck, Vicky."

"Thanks." Vicky picked up her rackets and went to the terrace. She knew Evelyn liked her and it pleased her. It would please Aunt Nan, too. But she knew what her father would say about their friendship. Evelyn would never be afraid of her. Respect her game, yes. But never fear her. And she didn't care.

Clifton had located court sixteen in the field, and he walked to it with her. "How do you feel?" he asked.

"Good—real good," she answered.

"Pace yourself," he warned. "The heat's in the 90's."

"I can tell it is." She ran her hand along her moist right arm and slid her finger around under the edge of her bandage. "I'll be all right. It's just as hot for her." She nodded toward her stocky opponent waiting for her at the gate.

Vicky found that the court was her haven. Everything faded into meaningless background except the length and breadth of the turf on which she was annihilating her opponent. She began to wish the girl was better so that she could play to conclusion her planned strategy for each point. But the nervous player on the other side faltered against the consistent length and pace with which Vicky pummeled the ball, and the match was over in twenty minutes.

Vicky played her first stadium match against Cecile Mercier in the round of sixteen. Walking down the marquee steps and across the grass to the farthest of the three courts with her opponent, she couldn't imagine how even Wimbledon could be more impressive than this. It looked to her as if the stadium were bursting at the seams with applauding spectators in colorful summer clothes. The flags hung limply above the rim in the muggy heat. The sun, beating down from a cloudless sky, made an oven of the enclosure. Vicky felt tense excitement in the atmosphere. And then, as the warm-up began, awareness of everything except the court and her job was gone.

She wondered what it was about the French girl's game that was dangerous. Granted steadiness and a smart tennis head, which anyone with her ranking should have, her strokes were so awkwardly produced that she seemed to be off balance when she made them. Her backhand, hit with the wrist and the back of her hand leading, looked like a beginner's effort at the stroke. There, Vicky thought, was the weakness to pound.

But as the match got under way, Vicky realized how misleading Cecile's form was. She made few errors. She hit hard on her backhand, despite her preposterous grip, and even harder on her forehand. And what she lacked in power on her volley, she made up for in placement. When they divided the first two games, Vicky read the warning: Don't underestimate her.

With the third game, she began to attack, seeing not Cecile and her odd strokes across the net, but a faceless victim whom she intended to sweep off the court. Hitting sharply angled drives that hugged the turf, she opened the court for winning volleys. And keeping the pace at fever pitch in the brutal heat, she saw her opponent begin to wilt. The strain of unorthodoxy, the lack of easy balance were telling on her. Mercilessly, Vicky attacked the French girl's serve, pounded her own wide to the corners; raked the court with flat and sliced drives and finished the point at the net. Cecile's defensive lobs shortened, her attempted passing shots grew weaker, and finally her resistance collapsed. Vicky had blazed her way into the semi-final where Jean Maguire, the number one American, waited for her.

In the welcome cool of one of the two stadium dressing rooms, Vicky got out of her wet clothes, took a shower, and lay down on the massage table to rest. The babble of voices outside grew louder and presently there was a knock on the door. The maid answered it and came back to her. "There're some reporters out there. They want to talk to you," she told Vicky.

"In a half hour," Vicky said, and knew, gratefully, that her father would be there then. He always gave her about forty minutes to shower and cool off and dress before he met her.

To her surprise, her father stood aside and let her handle the press herself. He was weaning her, she thought. Well, she was sure of the questions. They seldom varied. Did she think she could beat Maguire? She hoped she'd play well enough to win. Did the heat bother her? No. What did she think of Mercier's game? She's better than she looks. Then, realizing the risk of that reply, Her strokes are unorthodox, but she's good. Did she feel nervous playing in the stadium for the first time? "Did I look nervous?" she countered, and then her father stepped in.

"Will you excuse us now?" he asked pleasantly, not wanting a repetition of the Bagley article. "We have friends waiting for us." He took her tennis case in one hand, her arm with the other, and led her past the crowds at the refreshment stands and along the path toward the clubhouse.

"What friends, Dad?" Vicky asked, laughing.

"I had to say something," he grumbled as they went across the terrace and into the building. "How about a milkshake? You didn't eat much lunch."

They went to the empty dining room and sat at a table overlooking the field courts and the stadium. A waitress quickly took their order.

"That was a wonderful performance, Vicky." Clifton looked at her with affectionate pride. "I can tell you now, the odds were heavily against you, according to the papers. Experience and all that. You see how important it is not to know these things before you play?"

"It wouldn't have made any difference to me, Dad."

"I'm glad to hear it," he said, but she thought he doubted it. "Mercier looked like a set-up to me while you were rallying. Did she surprise you, too?"

"Yes," Vicky admitted. "At first. Her form's so terrible."

"When she began pasting the ball, I prayed you hadn't underestimated her as I did. I should have known you wouldn't."

"I don't know how she keeps from breaking her wrist on her backhand."

The waitress brought their milkshakes. When she had gone, Clifton asked, "Speaking of wrists, how does yours feel?"

"Fine. I'm going to leave the bandage off."

He nodded approvingly. "That's a good thing, psychologically too. Don't let them think it still bothers you. Your semi-final is Wednesday. You can have a light practice tomorrow without the bandage."

Vicky's eyes shifted from her father to the tall, slender girl in tennis clothes coming through the doorway from the terrace. "Chris!" she called, and the Californian turned a stormy face toward her.

"Oh—hi, Vicky," she said gloomily, but she managed a thin smile and came to the table. Clifton rose and greeted her.

"How did you do?" Vicky asked.

"I got clobbered," Chris answered, and flopped down on the chair Clifton pulled over for her, her rackets across her lap.

"Gee, I'm sorry." Vicky thought perhaps she shouldn't have asked. Chris looked beaten when she came in.

"That's too bad," Clifton sympathized, and sat down.

"Nell was seven feet tall today. I couldn't get anything past her."

"Would you like something to drink?" Clifton offered.

"No thanks. I drank a quart of orange juice after the match," she said. "I can't even think how to tell you to play her, Vicky, if you get in the final. She makes mistakes, but never on the points that count, and she hits like a ton. I don't think Evelyn Drury has a chance against her."

Vicky shook her head. "I don't either," she said. She'd seen Nell play. "Did you try to trade shots with her, Chris?" she asked.

"I guess I did. Stupid, wasn't it? But she won't let you play your game."

"She likes pace," Vicky remembered. "Would you practice with me tomorrow?"

Chris's eyebrows shot up. She looked at Clifton, then back at Vicky. "I thought you didn't—"

"Will you?" Vicky interrupted.

"Of course. What time?"

"Eleven. Then we won't miss any of the matches."

"I'll be here," Chris said, and got up. She gave Clifton's expressionless face a quick, uneasy glance and left them.

"I meant with the pro," Clifton snapped.

"I want to practice with her," Vicky answered.

"It's your show." He felt as if he had lost something and didn't know where to look for it.

"I wouldn't do it if there were a chance I'd play her in the tournament. But she's out of it," she went on, hoping to mollify him.

He said nothing until they had finished their drinks and got up to leave, and she suggested, "Let's watch the stadium matches."

"If you want to. I suppose you know enough not to tire

your eyes watching until the last dog's hung." He picked up her tennis case. "I'll leave this with the doorman."

She waited for him on the terrace, and when several minutes passed and he hadn't joined her, she went back into the clubhouse and saw him coming along, arm-in-arm, with Mary.

"Look who I found?" He beamed, letting go of Mary's arm as Vicky ran up to her and the two embraced.

"You kept your promise!" Vicky cried.

"Yes, but I'm so disappointed. I wanted to see you play today. I got caught up in the turnpike traffic. I thought I'd never get here." Mary held her off to look at her. "A semi-finalist in the Open! Vicky, I'm so proud of you. No need to ask how your wrist is."

"I saw her coming through the gate," Clifton said, and Vicky wanted to laugh at the complete change in his expression of a short while before. His eyes were positively dancing, his teeth gleamed in a broad smile, the lines of his craggy face softened.

Relieved, she said to Mary, "I'm awfully glad you came.

Mary seemed to know everyone in the marquee. McCord, meeting them on their way to the stands, invited them to sit in his box. The tournament chairman, the director, the president of the tennis association, several of the top ranking players and lesser officials, all greeted Mary during the course of the afternoon, and all of them congratulated Vicky on her win.

"You've got a lot of friends here," Vicky said, and realized that she had never associated Mary with any tennis but the juniors.

"I've known most of them for a long time," she explained. "I've been coming to Forest Hills for the semis and finals for years."

"Who's really the most important official?" Vicky asked.

Mary shrugged. "Their jobs are so interwoven here it's hard to say. Forest Hills was out of style for an Open this big. It needed a face-lifting—things like the new electric scoreboards and computer, the pavilions, the Open Club. The tournament director planned that, but he had to have the support of the president of the association and the cooperation of all the others—the tournament chairman, the West Side president and so on. You see—you just can't put your finger on one person. It's a big undertaking when you've got the best players in the world here." She put her hand on Vicky's. "As often as I've been coming here, I've never wanted anyone in particular to win, until now. You are going to win, aren't you?"

"I'll die trying," Vicky said.

That night, after the three of them had had dinner at the sidewalk cafe, the sky began to cloud over and the air grew even more sultry and oppressive than it had been during the day. Vicky excused herself, saying she was tired, and went to her room. Although she was a little tired after the excitement of the day, she really wanted to give them time to themselves. She thought her father was almost pathetic in his pleasure at having Mary here. He hadn't stopped smiling since she had arrived. He deserved it. It hadn't been easy for him, much of the time. She knew her injury had worried him far more than he had allowed her to know, and her matches here must have been a strain—he wanted so much for her to win. He had put his judgment on the line when he had predicted that she would and she supposed it was easier for her to play than for him to watch.

They didn't urge her to stay, and her father went to the elevator with her. "Get a good night's sleep, darling." He kissed her cheek. "If you want me, I'll be right down here in the lobby."

"Why don't you take Mary someplace?" she suggested. "It's no fun for her to sit in the lobby."

"You know I'm not going to leave here," he said.

"Well, have fun, anyway." As the elevator doors slowly closed, she saw that he was smiling again. No wonder Mary likes him so much, she thought. He sure is cool-looking when he's happy.

Notice of a telegram hung from the doorknob. Apprehensively, she pulled it off and took it to her room. No one would send her a wire about the quarter-finals. It's Aunt Nan, she cried to herself. Something's happened to her. And then she realized that the wire would have been sent to her father if that were so. She called the desk clerk and asked him to send it up to her, then sat on her bed to wait for it. The thought of Aunt Nan's being sick had given her a turn. What would they do if she were? Go home, of course. Aunt Nan was more important than the Open or anything else. She hoped she'd never have to be far from her for long.

A knock on the door brought her to her feet. She hurried to open it and took the telegram. Later she remembered that she should have tipped the bellboy but she closed the door quickly and tore at the flap of the envelope.

"Wonderful. Keep it up. The Marshes," she read.

She began to laugh. She laughed until tears came into her eyes, and then, catching sight of herself in the mirror above her bureau, she stopped and said to the reflection, "Have you flipped your lid?"

She propped the telegram against the lamp and turned

202

on the TV. "I'll bet Eddie made them do that," she thought, and she could see him as he had looked on Russian Hill, trying to get her to take his ring. She'd see him a lot again, when she got home and went to high school with him. She'd like that. She'd play tennis with him, too.

The next day, the dark clouds opened and the courts were flooded before the protective tarpaulin could be put over them. For two days it rained, and when the sun came out again, the matches were played on sodden, slippery turf.

Vicky had never seen a pair of "spikes." One of the players advised her to put socks over her tennis shoes when she played Jean Maguire, warning her not to try the leather shoes with short steel spikes since she wasn't used to them. So when she and Jean went on court for their match, following a man's quarter-final, she carried a pair of heavy white socks.

Vicky wished they were playing on the center of the three courts. The first court seemed so close to the marquee and the clattering typewriters, but as she looked around the horseshoe stadium, filled to capacity, at the TV cameras on their platform halfway up the stands, at the fluttering flags, and at a small plane droning high above them, she thought: Shut your mind to everything except this court and how you're going to use it.

She was certain, after the first two games, that Jean was way off form. She seemed more nervous than a champion should be, as if she were fearful of the slick court and the shots Vicky was forcing her to pursue on them. Or afraid of me, she said to herself. And as Jean's shots and her confidence faltered, so did her concentration. Only occasionally was there a flash of the brilliance that had won her a Wimbledon and an American championship, but Vicky kept alert for the sudden return to form that never came. It was necessary for her to do little more than keep her own errors to a minimum to win 6–2, 6–3.

The gallery exploded with excitement and the typewriters in the marquee seemed to go berserk. The applause thundered on while she put her sweater over her shoulders at the stand and received with outward calm the congratulations of linesmen and ballboys and the umpire, climbing down from his chair.

Ready to leave, she turned to Jean, almost forgotten in the excitement. "I'm sorry you didn't play your best today. I really am."

"I don't know why I was so bad. I felt all right," Jean told her, puzzled and disappointed. "But you were awfully good. I think you've got a chance to win it." She took Vicky's arm. "Come on, we've got to do the TV bit."

Vicky wasn't as nervous as she thought she'd be when the interviewer, moving them into position for the ground-level camera, began to interview her. But her voice sounded strangely unlike her own as she heard it echo back to her. Then Jean was interviewed and it was over. Vicky gave a little wave of her hand to her father and Mary, in McCord's box, and crossing the courts disappeared through the opening and went into the stadium dressing room.

"I don't want to see anybody, please," she told the maid. She had never before wanted so much to be alone. Not by a flicker of expression could the gallery or her opponent have had an inkling of the joy she felt at the mastery of her game today, and now she wanted the reward of thinking about it over and over in solitude. A thrill like an electric charge raced up her spine. One more—just one more. And she was at her peak, just as she needed it, as her father had planned it.

The walk from the stadium dressing room to the club-house seemed to Vicky the longest she had ever taken. Even her father and Mary, who met her at the dressing room door and flanked her protectively, could not stem the rush of autograph seekers, nor the press of reporters, who knew they had a story unmatched since the days of Maureen Connolly. "The youngest player ever to reach the semi-finals." That was a story in itself. This one sharpened the pencils of even the most unflappable press veterans: a four-teen-year-old disposes of the ranking American player and gets herself into the final—a David and Goliath match to be, if there ever was one. What apparently impressed them equally as much was Vicky's calmness about it all. Had they expected her to come dancing out of the dressing room, she wondered.

"You don't seem very excited. Did you expect to win?" one of them asked.

"I never expect to lose," she answered.

"How about Nell Stanley? Do you think you can beat her, too?"

A photographer ran in front of them and, walking back-ward, took several pictures with a small camera.

"I don't think you understood what my daughter meant," Clifton interrupted.

"Let her tell us," a reporter cut him off.

Vicky thought she knew what her father wanted her to clarify. "I never go on the court thinking I'm going to lose. That's what I meant," she explained.

"You shouldn't, of course," the reporter conceded. "But how are you going to play Stanley?"

Vicky gave him a quick smile. "That depends on how she plays me."

When the reporters left them at the terrace steps, Vicky said, "I want to go to my room. I've had it for now."

Clifton and Mary went up with her, and she stretched out on her bed. They talked quietly of her match, of the record she had set—the second in two seasons. "You have everything to win and nothing to lose now," Mary reminded her. But Vicky thought, I don't buy that, and she knew her father didn't either.

Toward evening, she was deluged with congratulatory telegrams from Aunt Nan, the Marshes, the tennis association, every California friend she had and, to her surprise, even from strangers. Clifton was kept busy going to the door for them. Mary opened them and handed them to Vicky who sat up on the bed and read them aloud.

And then the telephone began to ring. Chris and Evelyn and McCord, who hadn't had a chance to see her after her match, wanted to congratulate her and wish her good luck in the final. To her delight, the Tuckers phoned from Chestnut Hill to tell her how proud they were. Mary and her father talked to them, too, and no sooner had they hung up than Gwen Stuart called to tell her that everyone at the club was pulling for her.

"Let's get out of here," Clifton said when the phone rang again. "Let it ring."

"Where'll we go?" Vicky asked.

"To the Plaza for dinner. To the peace and quiet of New York," he laughed.

21 Vicky had a day's rest before the final. It was Mary who suggested that they get away from tennis, drive to the North Shore for lunch, and spend the afternoon in the country.

"But don't you want to see the matches?" Clifton asked.

"Not that much," Mary assured him.

So they went to Oyster Bay and had lunch and watched the sailboats on the Sound. And afterwards they drove along country roads until time to go back for dinner.

The next day Vicky felt refreshed by the change, eager for her match to begin.

The tension in the stadium was electric. Vicky looked neither to right nor left as she and Nell went down the marquee steps and onto the center court at two o'clock. Beside them walked the referee and the umpire, and behind them, in the blue-and-white draped VIP box, sat the Vice-President of the United States. Vicky shut her mind to it all, even the thunderous wave of applause sweeping the enclosure. This was probably the most important match she would ever play. She wanted to pretend she was playing it isolated from the reminders of BIG TENNIS.

Seeing her at a distance, Vicky had not realized quite how tall Nell Stanley was; but now, walking at the Australian girl's side, she felt dwarfed by her. There's a certain advantage to that, she thought. As she had noticed when she first saw her play, Nell had a long way to stoop for a shot and it could be tiring.

It was obvious from the start that Nell wasn't taking her lightly, and Vicky had a taste of the devastating power and depth that had annihilated the best women players in the world. Game after game went to the Australian before Vicky could begin to get into the match and discover the pattern of her opponent's placements that forced the opening for the deep, crushing, crosscourt forehand. Then, anticipating it, she took two games before Nell, at 5–2, on her service, slammed in two aces, made two ungettable volleys and the set was over.

The gallery seemed to have settled back to watch the inevitable conclusion. Their applause, a roaring of encouragement when Vicky won her two games, was appreciative of Nell's skill but restrained at the end of the set.

Vicky toweled off at the stand and took a sip of water. Over the rim of her cup, she glanced at Nell, who had the look of confidence and was barely perspiring. Then, slowly, she walked back to the baseline and took the balls the ballboy held out to her. For an instant she watched her opponent, bent over to receive service, legs ready to spring. And then she unleashed the power of her own game. Two serves flew by Nell untouched. The third and fourth forced weak replies that Vicky volleyed away for the game.

They changed sides on the odd game, and Vicky moved up inside the baseline to take Nell's serve. How often she had practiced this with Jerry Potter—blocking serves down the line or crosscourt to catch him at his feet as he came in. She didn't know why she had forgotten it in the first set, except that Nell hadn't given her much time to think. Three service returns in succession she hit straight at Nell's feet as she ran up. Crouching, volleying off her shoe tops, Nell found the net. Love-forty. She sliced a serve wide to the sideline hoping to force Vicky too far out of court to block the ball, and faulted, then double faulted.

Two–love. Vicky knew that all she had to do to win the set was to hold service. But that wasn't good enough. She wanted to shake her opponent's confidence, weaken her offense for the third set. Now that she held the upper hand, she saw that Nell, although still hitting powerfully, was not driving so close to the lines, and that she was tending to take the crosscourt opening rather than the pinpoint placement down the line. Anticipating this, Vicky was waiting for the ball, angling it off with decisive volleys. As she sensed her opponent's growing caution, she pressed her advantage. Going to the net on returns of serve as well as her own service, she punched for the deep corners. The low, sliding shots were forcing Nell almost to her knees and Vicky began to hear her tell-tale puffing.

Kept from the net, Nell's consistency in the backcourt was pushed to the limit. Uncharacteristic errors visibly annoyed her, and when Vicky won the set, 6–2, with a drop-volley that died on the court, she stood flatfooted for a moment, looking at the ball. Then she turned and walked off to the dressing room for the intermission. A storm of applause followed Vicky until she, too, had disappeared through the opening in the stadium wall.

Nell had taken the room on the right. Vicky went to her usual room on the left, quickly undressed and took a lukewarm shower. Evidently Nell was using the ten minutes to rest, for she didn't come into the shower room. She'll stiffen up, Vicky thought, but that was her headache.

Vicky put on fresh clothes and sat down to wait for the

knock on the door that would summon them back to court. Far from the let-down she had wondered if she would feel, she was exhilarated and eager to get on with the match. Every nerve in her body was keyed for the challenge, and she had a morale advantage in having won the second set.

There was a moment's applause when they returned to the court, and then an expectant hush fell over the stadium as Vicky started the third set with service. She was determined to give Nell no chance to get back on the overpowering game she had played in the first set. Serving fiercely with a single purpose—to force Nell wide of the court and volley deep into the opening on the other side—she took the first game at love. Nell struck back in the second, challenging Vicky desperately for the net position, carefully volleying the dipping returns for depth or angle. Surviving a volleying duel with Vicky that brought roars from the gallery, she evened the score.

Games seesawed to four-all, Vicky moving like a dancer, Nell running more heavily, obviously more tired. Vicky served wide, and as she ran in, Nell's forehand, crashing across court, passed her. She walked slowly back to the left court. This service game she *had* to hold. She couldn't let Nell regain her confidence, and a breakthrough would do that. Serving wide again and going up, she saw Nell's penetrating, sliced backhand flash down the line. Then she switched direction. Two services down the center line were aces and a netted return gave her the lead at 40–30. She served wide. The ball hit the chalk, sent up a little spray of white and took an erratic bounce away from Nell's racket in mid-swing. Awkwardly, Nell lobbed, but the ball was short and Vicky was ready for it. She sliced the smash off past the umpire's stand and led 5–4, match game.

Trying for an ace, Nell served a double fault. Vicky

slammed a backhand return down the line as Nell came up on her next serve to go ahead 30–0. For a moment Nell looked toward the marquee as if she were seeking encouragement from someone there. Vicky's eyes didn't move from her clearly nervous and distraught opponent. Nell turned her attention to the court again, took a deep breath, and flung her strong body into a serve. It was long. With scarcely a pause, she served again. The ball clipped the line, raised chalk, and sped on, too swiftly angled for Vicky to touch it. As Vicky bobbed her head to acknowledge the ace, the linesman yelled "out!"

Vicky looked at him. From across the court Nell stared at him. Surely he had called too quickly and would change his decision. Boos of protest rose from the gallery, and the umpire asked the linesman if he was certain of his decision.

The tight-lipped man swept his hand to the right, indicating a fault.

Nell looked appealingly to her friend in the marquee. Vicky shook her head and walked to the left court. She didn't want the point. It wasn't fair to get a triple match point lead that way. She had often been told that bad decisions evened up in the long run and never to throw a point. But this was different than a wrong call in a rally when the ball could be kept in play and the victim of the decision given a chance to win the point again. She was going to throw the point as inconspicuously as possible.

Nell served hard, but well within the sideline. She was taking no chance. Vicky swung at the ball and aimed below the net tape. The gallery applauded in approval she didn't want. Her face was an expressionless mask as she moved to the right court. Nell took a daring risk now. She blasted her serve wide to the sideline again. Unprepared, Vicky watched it go by and, before the linesman could make another mistake, strode quickly to the left court. One match point left, she thought, and she could see in her opponent's lightened step as she walked to position that her waning hope had been rekindled. This, Vicky told herself, is the point you *have* to win. She'll fight like a she-bear if she gets to deuce.

This one's for you, Jerry, Vicky said to herself as she moved up inside the baseline to take the serve. And when the speeding ball came to her backhand, she blocked it down the line past Nell and into the corner.

The stadium seemed to explode around her. Nell ran up to shake her hand wearily, and then at the stand linesmen were pumping her hand, patting her shoulder, all talking to her at once. She could scarcely hear what any of them said for the yelling, applauding gallery was giving her a standing ovation.

Nell sat in a chair by the stand, her weary head drooping, her hands resting on the racket handle between her knees, Vicky felt sorry for her and wished everyone would stop making such a fuss in front of her. But it went on, and suddenly Nell was there beside her. "You're a great player," she said, and her tired, dark eyes looked earnest when she added, "You deserved to win. My best wasn't good enough."

Vicky found her voice. "It's hard for you. I know I wasn't supposed to win."

Nell gave her a wry smile. "Frankly, I didn't think you'd get to the final. You're so young. How wrong can you be—" Her voice trailed off.

They were escorted to the first court for the presentation ceremony; the Vice-President was escorted from the marquee by a flanking bevy of officials, and the phalanx of photographers moved in. From midway up the stadium and from in front of them Vicky knew the television cameras would be recording this most gratifying and exciting moment of her life. Aunt Nan would be looking at it out in California. So would Eddie, she'd bet. And then a vision of Tony flashed in her mind. She could see those black, excited eyes glued to the television.

She hoped that she'd remember all the wonderful, flattering things the Vice-President was saying about her—things she had never expected to hear from someone so important.

And then she held a check for six thousand dollars in her hand, staring incredulously at the figure, and the ceremony was over for her.

Her father and Mary were waiting for her at the head of the marquee steps. Clifton was almost speechless. "Wonderful," was all he could say, but the pressure of his trembling arm around her waist told her how jubilant he felt. Mary kissed her hot cheek and gazed at her with misty eyes. Teasingly Vicky laughed. "Were you scared?"

"Not at all," Mary lied.

And then Vicky was engulfed by spectators and it was twenty minutes before she could make her way to the dressing room, with her father running interference through the crowd under the stadium.

She had showered and was sitting in her underclothes drinking orange juice when Jean Maguire and Chris burst into the room.

"You were the greatest!" Jean gave her a thump on the shoulder.

"Fantastic!" Chris looked almost as pleased as if she had won the match herself. "That last backhand!"

"Remember the day you showed me the grip?" Vicky asked.

"Little did I know," Chris laughed.

Vicky wondered if they were so pleased because Nell's triumphant march had been halted. And yet her own, she thought, had just begun.

"We came to talk to you about something," Jean said. "There wouldn't be a chance out there." She nodded toward the door. "That check you got for six thousand—you know the men's winner is going to get sixteen. Ten thousand more. And you were a bigger drawing card than anyone in the tournament. There's been a story about you almost every day in the papers."

"I don't read them during the tournament," Vicky said.

"Well, wait till you do," Chris smiled.

"And it's not just that," Jean went on. "Relatively, the women are as good as the men. A reporter took a poll for us. Seventy-six percent of the people he interviewed liked to see top women's matches as much as men's. Some enjoyed it more. And all of them thought a tournament without the women would be less interesting."

"So?" Vicky asked.

"We're going to fight for more equitable prize money. You know what the ratio is at the Pacific Coast International?"

Vicky shook her head. She hadn't even thought of it.

"Four to one for the men. Four thousand for the men's winner, one thousand for the women's. Even the men's runner-up gets two thousand. It makes us sick, and we're going to do something about it. Will you join us?"

Vicky looked at Jean's angry face. "I'll have to talk to my father about it."

"I guess you would," Chris said.

"There're a lot of us," Jean told her. "Most of the first ten feel this way. We've got to stick together."

"I'll talk to my father—really," Vicky promised, but she thought, Even though they're right, what a way to start out as Open champion, getting into a fight.

Finally alone with her father and Mary in her room, Vicky took her check from her purse and handed it to him "Isn't that something for a couple of hours work?"

"It's marvelous," Mary agreed.

"That's the result of two years hard practice and self-discipline, Vicky," her father reminded her. "And don't forget it. It'll make a nice start on a trust fund for you."

Vicky frowned at him. "Don't I get to spend any of it?"

"I'm still supporting you, with pleasure, and I'll buy you anything you want," he answered, then added, smiling, "within reason. But this is for your future, and there'll be a lot more to add to it by the time you're eighteen. Then you can think about what you want to do with it."

"Four years from now," she muttered.

"What irritates me," he said, putting the check in his wallet for safekeeping, "is the disparity in the men's and women's prize money—the downgrading of women's tennis. By God, you couldn't have seen a more exciting, finer match than you and Nell played today—or than Jean and Nell would probably play. You aren't second-class players—you're relatively the equal of the men."

"That's what Jean said," Vicky told him, and repeated as accurately as she could remember the conversation in the dressing room.

Clifton was thoughtful. Presently he said, "I've given our word you'll play in the Pacific Coast. It won't be easy for you—entering high school and having work to make up. And you'll have to play late matches. But I think you owe it to them. After that I have no objection to your taking sides on this, if you feel strongly enough about it to help right a wrong." He paused. "What do you think about it, Mary?"

"I don't know how they plan to do it, but if they do it with dignity, I'd fight like a steer for them," she replied.

"I guess it would be a cop-out if I didn't," Vicky decided.

Clifton had turned in his rented car, so Mary drove them to Kennedy Airport. Vicky looked forward to sleeping on the plane. All the excitement—the interviews, the picture-taking, the flood of telegrams and phone calls—that had followed her victory had been stimulating enough to keep her going at a swift pace. But a reaction had set in now and she felt "bone tired," as Aunt Nan would say. In her eagerness to board the plane when departure was announced, she scarcely noticed her father and Mary embracing, or his whispered words in Mary's ear. And as soon as the plane had taken off and she was permitted to tilt back her seat, she fell asleep.

Vicky was used to the homecoming celebration. There was nothing more they could do for her than they had done when she had won the national juniors. Aunt Nan had brought Tony to the airport this time, and without shyness he ran to her, yelling with delight, and she threw her arms around him, holding him in tight, grateful arms.

Aunt Nan, trying to be calm, gave up and let out a bleat of joy as Vicky went to her arms.

Only Eddie, approaching her slowly, seemed restrained.

"Well, aren't you glad to see me?" she asked. "Aren't you glad I won?"

"Of course I am. It's got to be the greatest—" He smiled a broad, loving, but awestruck smile.

"Then kiss me hello," she demanded, and Eddie happily obeyed.

It was two weeks later when Vicky came home from school to find her father already there, sitting at the window talking to Aunt Nan.

"What's the matter, Dad? Is something wrong?" she asked, alarmed.

"No, no. Pull a chair over, dear. I want to talk to you."

"Something awful's happened. I know it," she insisted, drawing a chair up beside him.

"Not awful—nice," Aunt Nan reassured her, and Vicky's anxious frown began to clear.

She gave her father a tentative smile. "Like you and Mary?"

"Yes." He looked at her intently. "I hope it won't upset you—"

"You're going to get married!" she blurted.

He nodded. "I'm flying back Wednesday."

"That's the day after tomorrow! Why didn't you tell me before?"

She was hurt. He could see it in her eyes and her tight, quivering mouth, and he took her hand to hold it tightly.

"Because I didn't know it myself," he explained. "I had to give her time to think about it. There's a lot involved for her, too. She phoned today. Her mother and father are going to Europe the first of October. She wants us to be married before they leave."

"Are you going to live back there?" Vicky asked in a small voice.

"Of course not. Do you think I'd leave you? We're

having a small wedding at the house on the twenty-seventh
—that's the way she wants it. Then we'll have a short
honeymoon and I'll bring her out here."

"Here?" Vicky cried.

"Not to this apartment. You and Mary and I are going
to have one not too far from Aunt Nan, with a beautiful
view of the bay. I have an agent working on it, and you and
Aunt Nan can help."

Vicky got up and perched on the arm of Aunt Nan's
chair. She put an arm around her shoulders. "I can stay
with Aunt Nan whenever I want to, can't I?"

"Any time," he promised. "And Aunt Nan's going to be
your tennis companion from now on."

Vicky didn't want to show too much pleasure, but she
knew it was time for her father to let go of the reins. "Will
you like that, Aunt Nan?" she asked.

"I hope I'm up to it," Aunt Nan said.

"You have the horse sense, Nan. I've just provided the
drive."

"Just!" Aunt Nan laughed.

"I couldn't have won without you, and you know it,
Dad," Vicky told him.

"Thank you, darling. But you can now. And Wimbledon, too." He smiled gently at her. "You'll find things
about your game you'll want to improve as long as you
play. But you've got everything else. I've seen that, Vicky."

Vicky looked at him soberly and silently for a moment.
Then she left Aunt Nan's side and sat down on his lap. She
put her arms around his neck and her cheek against his, and
he held her closely for a long time. He tried to remember
when she had last done this. She must have been four or
five, he thought.

Early Wednesday morning, they stood at one of the air terminal windows, Aunt Nan and Vicky, watching the plane grow smaller as it winged through a clear blue sky over the Oakland hills.

"I feel like he's going away forever."Vicky spoke almost inaudibly.

"He'll be back before you know it," Aunt Nan said. "In the meantime we've got a job to do for him."

"I didn't mean that."

With a final silver flash the plane disappeared.

"Whatever you're thinking, you'll always come first with him," Aunt Nan told her."Anyway, there's a lot of him to share. The only thing that worries me is the thought of trying to fill his tennis shoes."

"You don't have to," Vicky said. "I'm grown up now."

Aunt Nan smiled tenderly at her serious face. "So the papers say."

They walked back through the long corridors and out of the building to the parking lot.

About the Author

Helen Hull Jacobs was born in Arizona, grew up in San Francisco and Berkeley, and attended the Anna Head School for Girls and the University of California at Berkeley. Winning the National Junior Tennis Championship when she was sixteen and seventeen and the United States Women's Singles Championship four times in succession, Miss Jacobs went on to win the world's tennis championship at Wimbledon, England. She was inducted into the National Lawn Tennis Association's Hall of Fame in 1962.

Miss Jacobs began writing about the tennis world when she entered it herself and has continued to write in her home in East Hampton, New York.